The
Last Summer

The
Last Summer

Mary Rose Callaghan

POOLBEG

Published 1997 by
Poolbeg Press Ltd
123 Baldoyle Industrial Estate
Dublin 13, Ireland

© Mary Rose Callaghan 1997

The moral right of the author has been asserted.

The Publishers gratefully acknowledge the support of
The Arts Council.

A catalogue record for this book is available from the British Library.

ISBN 1 85371 607 3

Cover design by Poolbeg Group Services Ltd
Set by Poolbeg Group Services Ltd in Goudy 10.5/14
Printed by The Guernsey Press Ltd,
Vale, Guernsey, Channel Islands.

Also by Mary Rose Callaghan

Mothers
Confessions of a Prodigal Daughter
Kitty O'Shea, A Life of Katharine Parnell
The Awkward Girl
Has Anyone Seen Heather?
Emigrant Dreams

About the Author

Mary Rose Callaghan was educated in UCD. She has worked as a teacher and was assistant editor of *The Arts in Ireland* magazine. In 1975 she emigrated to America, where she lived for nearly twenty years. She now lives in Bray, County Wicklow, with her husband, Robert Hogan. Her first novel with Poolbeg, *Emigrant Dreams*, was published in 1996.

With thanks to all at Poolbeg Press,
especially my editor, Kate Cruise O'Brien.

*This book is for Robert James,
with thanks for inspiration.
Also thanks to my niece,
the other MRC, for advice.*

Chapter One

The day after the Leaving I awoke to Dad's singing. It came from the kitchen where he was making breakfast. The sun was shining outside, the exams over and my whole life ahead. But I lay there, feeling wormy.

Then I remembered – Heather was pregnant.

Heather's our mum.

And forty-three.

Hell, the daughter's usually up the pole. Our family was always in reverse. Heather's hormones must've gone screwy. Or else the parents were sexfiends. It was weird – for years they'd done nothing but yell at each other. Now this.

Katie snored obliviously beside me.

We shared the room. And the big double bed. Sisters are supposed to be cheerful about sharing, but not us. The bed was like a bucking bronco – if Katie moved I was hoisted up. And vice-versa. You spent the night clutching the edge. There was no choice as our house only had two bedrooms. It was a rented bungalow off the Sidmonton Road in Bray. The wallpaper was peeling. And there was no bath, only a shower which I hated.

Otherwise it was OK. So long as you got up early to avoid

Katie. Lately she fought all the time. Everything and everyone was boring. She was another one in hormonal hell, which was putting it kindly. If Heather had a girl, it'd start all over again. I'd be coping with teenagers at thirty.

I couldn't doze, so tiptoed out to the kitchen. It was dank and there were cold quarry tiles on the floor. Dad was doing his Al Jolson number:

> I'd walk a million miles,
>
> for one of your smiles,
>
> My Ma-ha-hammy . . .

Dad's from Tallahassee, Florida. And, like most Americans, a morning person. Although last to bed, he was always up first. He'd already been to the corner shop in his dressing-gown and slippers for the paper. The neighbours thought this habit crazy. Maybe it was. It was certainly crazy to be so cheerful now.

"Morning, Clare." His eyebrows went up, giving him his innocent look.

I flicked on the radio. "Hi, Dad."

He clattered around, taking up psychic space. He's an actor and still fit and handsome – for forty-six. A William Hurt look-alike, except for his dyed brown hair. It was thinning a bit at the front, but baldness is a sign of virility, according to Heather – from too much testosterone. It must make men impractical too. Something had certainly made him like that. He was currently in a failing play – the story of his life.

I made tea, concentrating on the news.

Then came *It Says in the Papers*. It was hard to hear anything with Dad's din.

> My dear, old Ma-ha-hammy . . .

Mammy? His own was dead.

Did he mean Heather? Maybe he liked mammies and babies? It had made me regress – last night I'd eaten a whole

packet of Marietta biscuits and gone to bed with a book
Tales of Avonlea, which I've read millions and millions of
times.

Who'd look after a baby?

Me.

Who else? Where'd it sleep? And what would Grandfather
say? He'd already brought up Katie and me.

It was the last Mohican. Yet Dad had bought Heather a
rose to celebrate and she had calmly started knitting booties.
That's when she wasn't devouring her romantic novels which
were scattered all over the house. She liked books about
finding Mr Right – men with blazing eyes and twitches in their
steely jaws.

Dad had a twitch OK, but it usually meant an explosion.

He flip-flopped around, his tartan dressing-gown just over
his bony knees, his hairy chest bare as he slammed plates on
the table. It was OK to cook breakfast, but no other meal.
"Sleep well, Clare?"

I nodded.

"Eggs?"

"No thanks."

I hated eggs, although two a week are recommended. Two's
the magic number – it's red meat twice-weekly, two glasses of
red wine daily, and two-by-two into the Ark. Wally, my
boyfriend, had just gone to the States for the summer, so for
the present the Ark was out for me. And wine was an absolute
no for our family. Firstly, no money, and secondly, Dad's an
alcoholic – retired.

His play had got bad reviews, so no one was coming –
audiences are a problem in Dublin. Although you could never
tell from Dad. He was always cheerful. Or else pretending to
be. He wanted to make the big time. The more hopeless

something was, the more the challenge. He was stage-struck and I got it from him.

"The Stillorgan Road is crawling all the way into Dublin. The centre city is moving slowly. The Rock Road is solid," announced *AA Roadwatch*.

I was imagining this phenomenon when Dad snapped it off – an irritating habit of his.

"Toast, Clare?"

"No thanks."

"Whatja eatin'?"

I shrugged. "Cereal."

"Dreaded wheat?" His idea of a joke.

I sipped my tea. A Roddy Doyle paperback was propped before me. That way, I didn't have to talk. Anyway I can't in the morning. I can barely manage to eat cereal. Whereas Dad talks his head off and lashes down grapefruit, greasy fries, and heaps of white toast or pancakes. Just about everything bad. I worry about him getting strokes, so suggested kippers, another recommended twice-weekly, for the Omega 3 factor. But he wouldn't hear of it – they stank the whole house.

We ate till about Tuesday. Then it was porridge or spaghetti and ketchup, till Heather got paid on Fridays. I was semi-vegetarian since mad cow disease, so didn't mind. And Katie grazed on coke and crisps.

Heather came in then, beaming at Dad. She was a petite blonde. Her hair was more sandy now, but the fringe made her seem younger. She hadn't begun to show anything yet, but had that peachy glow. You know that smug, pregnant look?

"Sleep well, darling?" she asked Dad.

He frowned. "Till about six."

"Oh, poor darling," she cooed, then turned to me. "You're up early, Clare?"

I nodded sleepily.

Heather concentrated on Dad. She'd do anything for his approval. At least she no longer depended on him financially. She was her own woman now, and already dressed prettily for her job in the bookshop, where she was their expert on Mills and Boon. I suppose, type-wise, she's a Felicity Kendal – ageing innocence, with a conviction, like all the Irish, that she'll win the Lottery. She said it was in her long-term horoscope, another thing she read religiously.

Now she pouted at Dad. "I didn't hear you come in."

He grabbed her bum. "I was out gallivantin'."

It was revolting – first thing in the morning.

As they hugged and laughed, I looked the other way.

Hell, she was perimenopausal. What age did you get the *real* menopause anyway? And didn't the sexual drive *ever* go? Obviously not in her case. Age didn't stop Dad either. He'd given her a saucepan for their twentieth anniversary. A saucepan? Imagine anything more unromantic? I thought it downright barbaric. But he said it was the triumph of hope over experience, as Heather hardly ever cooked and I have to admit we needed it. The house wasn't well supplied. There were only a few burnt out aluminium pots, in the bottom of a musty old dresser. There was hardly any matching delph. Nothing had been changed since the thirties and the kitchen had nasty smells, especially under the huge enamel sink.

Heather held both hands teasingly behind her back. "Which hand, darling?"

Dad looked puzzled. "A letter?"

"From America. It came yesterday." She walked backward playfully. "Now, guess!"

Of course, he picked the wrong one.

She gave him the letter anyway.

He put her fry on the table, glancing curiously at the envelope.

She looked queasy. "I'll skip the egg."

"Sit! You're eating for two." He pushed her down.

God.

He ripped the envelope open.

I poured some cardboard flakes. I'd read in one of the Sundays that sex was out for two years with a baby. You didn't feel like it before the birth, and afterwards you were too exhausted. Why'd they been so careless? Had Heather been afraid to refuse? A man would *never* push me around. Or make me eat eggs.

"Well, girls. We're having a visitor," Dad announced matter-of-factly.

We "girls" looked at each other.

"When, darling?" Heather smiled dippily.

A visitor?

Damn.

Dad scanned the letter. "Luke, my army buddy's, coming to Dublin."

"Luke Merrill, the academic?" Heather's mouth was full of brekky.

He looked up. "Yeah, the guy in the University of Delaware . . ."

"'What did Della wear?'" Heather sang, "'What did Del-a-a-wear?' Remember that, Dan?"

"'She wore a bright, new Jersey. O-oh . . . that's what she did w-e-e-ar,'" he crooned back.

And they both fell about giggling.

God. What was so funny?

When Dad recovered, he read the back of the page. "Hmm . . . he's researching Boucicault for the summer . . ."

I looked over. "Who's Boucicault?"

Dad frowned. "You've seen *The Shaughraun*, Clare."

"Yeah." It was in the Abbey a few summers back.

"He wrote it."

"Oh."

I hummed a tune from acting class – we sang it to the rhythm of *Knees Up, Mother Brown*.

> Danger, men at work
> Danger, men at work
> Danger
> Danger
> Men at work, danger
> Danger, men at work . . .

Someone researching a playwright couldn't be *all* bad. But, like the baby, a visitor was a coffin-nail in our new-found happiness. For years my sister and I'd been farmed out in Ranelagh with our grandfather and grandaunt, Brigid, while the parents gallivanted in London. I used to tell everyone that Dad was acting in Stratford and the Royal Court, but he only had small provincial parts in places like Maidenhead and Maidstone. Now we were all back together. A few months ago, the parents said we girls *needed* them, and came home.

Just like that.

It was tautology to say we needed them. We always *had* for God's sake. And, after so many years, Katie and I were still reeling with the shock.

Our little house was in Westfield Park, an enclave of bungalows, just up from the seafront. It was from seedier days, built in the thirties, Dad said, for British army widows. There were old ladies in some of them – who didn't look remotely British. But Dad gets these ideas. He says people want to live in Ireland because it's cheaper – he never goes shopping, so how would he know? Our house was called Haworth, and there was a Hareton, Hindley and Heathcliff on the other side, a definite Yorkshire motif. The builder or someone must've been fond of the Brontës – they're OK, but not Jane Austen.

Still, Haworth was an unusual name, and the house was full of old unusual furniture. The garden had high green hedges and apples and raspberries in the back. The hedges made things dark, but I liked the privacy. Also hearing the sea at night. And looking at the stars. The old lady owner was in a nursing home on the Meath Road. I felt sorry about her but glad about us. Although in need of repair, the bungalow was home – what we'd always wanted. But would our happiness be built on sand, with another sibling on the way?

Katie and the parents were enough.

And now Luke What's-his-name was coming.

The parents chatted obliviously, Dad recalling first meeting Luke in a dire Alabama boot camp. They were both drafted for Vietnam and suffered through basic training together. Then Luke had got off base by marrying someone he'd met at a dance. Of course, he was divorced now. Twice. Everyone in America was.

"Will he be staying long?" I asked pointedly.

Dad peered back at the letter. "A month, maybe two. He's vague. Just says – the summer."

A month?

Maybe two?

The summer?

God.

"He might prefer a B & B," I suggested tactfully. Every second house in Bray had a B & B sign. In between there were old people's homes.

Dad's bald bit wrinkled. "Ah, no, sweetheart. He's my buddy."

I couldn't imagine my dad with buddies. Like something out of Forrest Gump. There were snaps of him in goofy US army camouflage fatigues with his head shaved like a concentration camp victim. Others showed him in a dressier uniform, looking young and sweet. His past was sort of exotic, except he'd killed for his country. Which had caused his drinking. At least, that's what he said. They all blame something. Or someone.

"Well, we've plenty of space." Heather didn't seem to mind the prospect of an invasion.

Plenty of space? Was she cracked? We were bursting out of the house. A guest would have to sleep on the lumpy couch. Which meant we couldn't use the sitting-room. And I didn't ask the obvious – had he a big appetite? If so, he was likely to go hungry. Maybe he liked porridge. Or Heather's spaghetti. As kids, she told us her recipe was unique. That no one could cook like her – as she poured ketchup over the glutinous mess. Idiotically we believed her. Parents can tell you anything – up to a certain age.

Now, while Dad leafed through the paper, she was deep in a new novel. I munched flakes, staring at the salacious cover. How could she read that stuff?

"How'd it go last night?" I asked Dad

"Oh, the usual." He shrugged. "We're dogging a fled horse."

His habit of swopping letters is from some US comic. So "absolutely beautiful" becomes "boobsolutely abuful." A "boob"'s anything good.

Copycat Katie went round calling things "boobs," which nobody understood. Her other word's "cool." Which Heather said was making a come-back. Things were "cool" in her day too.

My sister, the Sleeping Beauty, came in then, dressed in her usual arctic sweats. Her long blonde hair was tangled and she was rubbing blackened eyes. She's all legs and hair and about five, eight. A hurricane with red lips and creamy skin. She'd inherited Heather's colouring and Dad's height, while I was dark like him and squat like Heather.

Katie yawned and made for the teapot.

I waited for Dad to do his bit – ask sternly what time she'd got in. It was midsummer's night and she'd been at a cider bash on the Esplanade.

He just blinked benignly. "How was the party, sweetheart?"

Typical.

And nothing about drinking cider. Some way to bring up kids.

"A boob," Katie groaned.

There, she'd said it.

Then, stretching and yawning again, "We had a barbecue."

Even Heather smiled. "You should sleep in, Katie. You were so late."

So she'd noticed. It wouldn't be long till they irked each other. They rowed all the time these days – especially before Katie got the curse. She was like a maniac then with PMT.

"You're still growing, Katie," Dad chipped in.

Did he want her any taller? She already had six inches on me. And if she needed rest, couldn't she go to bed earlier?

She was spoilt.

Dead spoilt.

I went back to my book.

A sixteen year old shouldn't be allowed to roam Bray by night. People got attacked all the time. The parents knew nothing. Not even what they were in for with a baby. I had experience of baby-sitting. It'd need things – a cot, clothes, etc.

10

Oh, Dad scraped up the rent. And I suppose Heather could work for a few months more. But what then? I was unemployed. There were no jobs for me in Bray. Katie, of course, hadn't even looked. Oh, I had the offer of au-pairing in France, but we'd only just got the bungalow. I couldn't possibly go.

Then Dad said, "Enjoying Roddy Doyle, Clare?"

He'd given it to me, so I had to be careful. Unlike Heather, Dad was a serious reader and hooked on Oscar Wilde. He liked all writers with a sense of humour and had really enjoyed the *Commitments* film.

"He's not Shakespeare," I said.

He sipped his coffee. "Few writers are."

I sighed. "They're thinking of putting him on the Leaving."

"Well, that'll liven things up."

I said nothing.

"Part of the new multi-culturalism, Clare. Don't you approve?" Dad quizzed me in mock irritation.

"The multi-what?"

"The swing against western male dominance – Dead White Males. Surely, you agree with that? As a feminist?"

Dad didn't like feminism. "He's a living white male."

"And a new voice. He writes about ordinary Dubliners – that's refreshing. And there's more emphasis on women writers now." His voice was placating.

"I prefer Shakespeare."

He laughed. "You're in a minority, pumpkin."

My heart missed a beat. Dad hadn't called me that for absolutely years. It was a southern fruit, but stirred God-knows-what memories. I was tennish when he left Heather. Just walked off to London, and of course she'd followed like one of those Boyzone fans. Although we went for holidays, they'd stayed for years, dumping us in Ranelagh.

11

"Hmm . . . most kids your age have never even seen Shakespeare," he went on.

"Hope I never have to." Katie's mouth was full.

My sister's limited – it'd be a different story if Shakespeare had played soccer. Or was a member of *Oasis*.

"Nonsense," Heather said. "I saw Anew MacMaster in school."

Dad grimaced. "That ham?"

Heather smiled dreamily. "Oh, he wasn't bad."

I thought she only liked Cliff Richard – terrible things like "Livin' Doll." And Elvis, singing "Wooden Heart." They were even before her time.

"Was it the Dark Ages?" Katie tried to be funny – another habit of hers.

"It was around 1960," Heather went on. "He did scenes from the tragedies. They let the juniors in."

How could anyone even *remember* that far back? And here she was expecting again. "That's over thirty-five years ago," I said slowly.

Heather fiddled with her wedding ring. "I suppose it must be."

"Pre-history," Katie quipped.

Heather looked hurt.

Dad glared.

"I can't joke?" Katie plonked her elbows rudely on the table. It hadn't taken her long to argue. You can usually time it.

"I didn't say that!" Heather was red in the face.

"You did!" Katie grumped.

"Well, I'm *sorry*, Katie."

"You always pick on me!"

12

"I've *said* I'm sorry," Heather placated.

Heather was always apologising. Her fatal flaw.

"Why should *you* be sorry?" I snapped.

"Please, girls!" Dad looked up from the paper. He always called us this. He threatened to found a society called MANG –*Men Against Nagging Girls*.

"It's their hormones," I added.

His eyebrows went up. "What?"

"Perimenopausal women and teenage girls have the same hormonal imbalance."

Heather reddened. "Clare, please . . . "

"It was in *Time* magazine." I insisted.

"Could we talk about something else at breakfast?" Dad rustled the paper.

Heather patted her tummy smugly. "I couldn't be peripausal yet, Clare."

"Perimenopausal!"

"Clare!" Dad yelled.

"It's censorship now?"

"I asked you to talk about something else!"

"I'm talking to Heather!"

Our eyes met. She rolled hers heavenward.

It meant: "I'm on your side." He was always picking on me, whereas Katie got away with murder. I was about to ask why he grabbed Heather's bum, if the rest of her body wasn't fit for discussion, but he glared me into silence.

Heather broke it. "Well, I'm off! Remember the bins, Clare." Then she kissed Dad, grabbed her book and knitting and dashed.

She should be knitting for grandkids.

Not that I was ready to oblige on that front. Who ever

heard of being peripausal? It sounded like something wrong with your heart.

I suddenly felt protective. Lately Heather had started night classes to improve her English. Dad jeered this, saying the class was useless. But she wanted to write better, and didn't even know how to plan her thoughts ahead. She said she'd missed out on English at school. If you ask me, she'd missed out on a lot of things. And she couldn't cope with kids, because she was one. At her age would it be OK? Women still died in childbirth.

As we lingered over breakfast, Dad sat frowning. A sign of deep thought. Then he made more coffee.

"Clare," he said slowly. "Anew MacMaster's given me an idea."

Alarms went off in my head.

"'What's the key to success?'" Katie repeated a stupid riddle from a Christmas cracker. "'First fill your head with ideas, then shoot!'"

She collapsed into laughter.

She did this all the time. Laughed at her own jokes.

Dad ignored her. "Clare," he went on seriously. "You read *Hamlet* for your test?"

"Yeah."

He always called the Leaving this. I told him it was more than a test. It was your fate, your destiny, your WHOLE DAMN LIFE.

He rubbed his ear ominously. "Ever see it performed?"

"Oh, the school rented a video. The Laurence Olivier."

"Old hat!" Dad whistled, punching his forehead. "I've got a brainwave!"

God, not another one. His brainwaves were always

14

disasters. As I said, his present play was threatening to close. Even Katie looked nervous.

"What?" we said together.

"Joe Papp put on Shakespeare in Central Park," Dad mused.

"We have the Green," Katie piped up.

Dad's eyes gleamed. "Exactly!"

". . . and the Irish weather," I added.

"But it's summer now," Katie pleaded. "Maybe a play about summer!"

Dad whistled. "A *Midsummer Night's Dream*. Hey now."

"There'd be parts for us." I joined in the fantasy.

Katie grimaced. "Shakespeare's boring. And not even English!"

Now I'd heard it all. "It is English."

"It's not! It's worse than Latin," my sister went on.

Her ignorance was bottomless.

As Dad brooded on, I wondered if he'd give me a part? After all I'd done a foundation course in acting last year. We did voice training – resonance and projection. And all kinds of breathing exercises. I could extend my diaphragm and hold my breath for five minutes. I had even taken part in the Feis.

"It'd be too costly," I said finally.

Dad got up and left the room. "Anything can happen, Clare."

He said this a lot.

It was a bad sign.

He got the same look in his eye when he tried to make videos once. The camera was now in hock. And last year he'd started a travel agency that specialised in foreign theatre

15

festivals. It flopped when a plane broke down in Iceland. It didn't make sense. If you couldn't get people to the theatre in Dublin, how would they ever go there? And would anyone in Ireland be bothered with outdoor Shakespeare? They didn't even like it indoors.

We never found out.

But that breakfast was the start of another midsummer night's madness. What's in the womb of time will be delivered, and there was more than Heather's baby trying to get born.

Chapter Two

Dad's play closed that week.

It was by some woman he was trying to help – an unknown writer. But a good play, he said, murdered by the media. I'd laughed all through it, yet *The Irish Times* panned it. All the papers did, except one evening paper, which said it was the "most refreshing thing on this year." Reviewing was a joke in Dublin – it was part of the general world decline. The papers sent out hacks who have no sense of humour and knew damn all about the stage. Another thing, I was to learn that summer.

With Dad on the dole, we were pretty depressed. He had a bad case of USD – Unemployment Stress Disorder. At least he'd stopped talking about producing Shakespeare. It was a fantasy on my part that I could be in it. I wasn't a dreamer like him – that was for sure. It'd only be another of his turkeys – which, by the way, are nothing to do with talking, or Christmas.

We had a family conference and decided on economies – Katie was to give up coke and Dad cigarettes. But he was home all the time now – sneaking them. They smelt-up the bathroom and the sitting-room in the morning – even though he opened all the windows so that the place was like a

17

draughty railway station. If I said anything, he just yelled that he was definitely founding his society, which now became FANG – *Fathers Against Nagging Girls*. Katie was just as bad. She stole his cigarettes and smoked secretly too – when she wasn't being bored or talking in riddles.

Heather kept on knitting calmly. She said all our long-term horoscopes were good, so things were bound to change. It was only a matter of time. If we were poor before, we were now on our uppers. Oh, Heather's measly salary kept us fed, but there was no money for Lottery tickets and, with no hope of winning, nothing to look forward to. If Dad didn't get work soon, we'd be living totally on Heather's spaghetti and ketchup. So I read up low cost recipes, and bought a sack of potatoes just in case.

Mostly I went around worrying.

Dad went around saying, "I'll think of something, girls".

The "girls," as always, included Heather.

Nothing fazed her. She smiled her dippy smile, now on her second bootie, while Dad hung around the house, thinking up mad schemes. He couldn't phone anyone, because there was no phone, as we hadn't the deposit. As usual, while he talked in millions, we were almost penniless. His latest plan was to start a new video rental company in Bray for artistic and foreign movies. There were already three video shops in Bray, which he didn't seem to have noticed. My dad was dedicated to the arts – especially the performing arts. But this was ominous. Generally we were getting on each other's nerves.

For years I'd prayed that he and Heather would come home. By the time they actually did, I'd given up – which gave me serious doubts about religion. Now we were together again, but I'd imagined it all so differently – like something out of Jane Austen: The family of Kelly had long been settled in

Wicklow. Their estate was large and their residence was at Westfield Park, where, for many generations, they had lived in so respectable a manner, as to engage the general good opinion of their surrounding acquaintance. . .

But life wasn't a book.

I knew that.

Would it be back to the grandfather farm in Ranelagh? And a life of looking in other people's windows. When we lived with Grandad, Katie and I always roamed Ranelagh after school, sometimes as far as Palmerston Park, spying. Looking in windows was our favourite hobby. You know that lovely twilight hour before the curtains are drawn and the lights are low? Inside, children are staring at TV, or being helped with homework. Everyone had mothers and fathers – that's everyone else.

Now we did.

But, as I said, it wasn't what we expected.

It was getting like the old days when Dad shouted. He shouted so much when we were little that Trout left. Trout was our dog – Katie's dog really. We were living in a flat in Ballsbridge, so Dad said he was stolen by the Spring Show crowd, but he ran away. I know. There was too much fighting in our house.

To pass the time I read Shakespeare. *King Lear* reminded me of our grandfather – a stubborn old man who fought with his daughters. Except in Grandfather's case, there was only one: Heather. Lady Macbeth was a she-devil, but you felt sorry for her when she became a psychiatric patient. *Hamlet* wasn't mad, he just needed a course in decision-making.

In between I exercised my resonators: humming for the lips; chanting MEEM, MAIM, MINE, MOHN, and NEEN, NAIN, NINE, NOHN for the nose; and HAH, HOW, HOY, and WAH, WOW, WOY for the throat. I'd had an interview for Drama Studies, and an audition for the Acting Diploma at the Beckett Centre in Trinity. I was hoping for a recall any day, yet there was no guarantee they'd pick me for either.

"W-A-A-H . . . W-A-A-H . . . – I intoned one day as Dad ran frantically into the house.

"W-A-A-H . . ."

"Oh, shit! Clare! Clare!" He was staring at his feet.

"What is it?" Had he broken a toe or something?

"Look!" He pointed down in disgust.

"What?" I couldn't see anything.

"My shoes!"

"What about them?" They were worn white Nikes.

He balanced on the sides of the shoes. "Shit!"

"What's wrong?"

"Shit!"

I stared at them.

"Do something, Clare!"

"What *is* it?"

"It's shit! I stepped in dog *shit*! Can't you see?"

It was hardly noticeable, nothing. "Is that all?"

He was outraged. "Clare!"

"Go out to the garden and wipe your feet on the grass," I said calmly.

He ran out the back door, yelling at me to follow.

I held the shoes under the garden tap.

Honestly, who'd believe it? A grown man. How long did it take to get over things? The Vietnam War was pre-history, at least pre-Katie and me. We weren't even thought of then. How long did we have to tiptoe around him? Oh, Bray's bad in places for dog dirt. What did he expect? Them to go constipated, because he wouldn't look where he was going? It's

20

a free world, after all, and animals live here too. When I told Dad this, he yelled that it was a very expensive world.

Amazing, he'd noticed.

He'd started counting his cigarettes, so maybe he was getting more observant. He went on about other things too. If he lost anything, you had to drop everything and find it immediately. Heather's night class seemed to incense him more and more. He acted like some kind of jealous sultan because she was improving herself. What did he think she was doing there – with her bump growing daily? And he complained about the laundry piling up into Himalayan heaps. One day he threw a fit about no clean socks. As there was no bathtub and no money for the launderette, Katie and I did it in the old kitchen sink.

Heather kept saying to be patient.

It was dangerous, men working, but even worse when they weren't. The last time Dad was unemployed he'd started drinking and hitting Heather. That's how they ended up in London for all those years. And now what about the baby? And my college plans? Katie still had school, while my heart was set on Trinity – it's a cliché, I know, but there's no other way to say it. My heart was set.

Days passed and no interview recall.

I practised my audition pieces: Portia's plea for mercy, and a modern one from *Dancing at Lughnasa*. I learnt an extra monologue from *Faith Healer*– about a sad woman who suffered a stillbirth.

I did my breathing exercises. And recited a ditty for my diction:

> Down by the Merseyside,
> Playing on the bandstand,
> John Paul George and Ringo Starr

21

> Started as a skiffle group
> Then made the bigtime
> Found they could only go so far.

I'd learnt it in acting class.

I'd wanted to act from the year dot – age three actually – and fancied myself as another Fiona Shaw, some sort of living legend. But things were looking grim now. Even if I got a college place, would I get a grant? Free fees were coming in, but that hadn't happened yet. If not, how could I pay for lunch, transport, etc.? I planted some lettuce and thought up ways of making money. I encouraged a tomato plant in the garden. At best it would only produce ten tomatoes. Not enough for a catering business. The raspberries were hopelessly small. The garden was too dark. If I could get them to grow, I could make jam, or cakes or something, but that was like one of Dad's cracked schemes. Or I could take up grandfather's offer of being his paid gardener instead of unpaid one.

No. Taking money from Grandfather was the last Mohican. He was too old.

Dad grumbled about him driving. He said eighty-five-year olds were a menace on the roads. Maybe it was true. Last week grandfather had gone through a red light. And the week before, he'd pulled out in front of a bus. Dad was afraid he'd kill himself or someone else, and suggested crazy things like stealing his car keys. Or letting the air out of the tyres. Grandfather was too stubborn to take advice. He never listened to anyone.

Now he was mad because I refused to au-pair in France. He'd paid my fare last year, and I spent an OK month in Toulouse. Except I was homesick for Katie's stupid jokes. Of course, Grandfather'd forecast a lifetime's regret. The parents didn't mind and gave me busfare to look for work in town.

They were good about that. They never made us do anything. But, so far, no luck.

So it was back to baby-sitting.

Katie, as usual, sponged off me.

Things got worse.

Then Luke came.

One July morning his taxi stopped outside our house. Heather had gone to work and we were all still in a state of *dishabille*. Dad saw him at the gate from the window and ran up the garden path in his skimpy tartan dressing gown. "Well, son of a gun!"

"Dan!" Luke had a funny Texas drawl. He had a peppery beard but was younger-looking than Dad because of his thick wavy hair. And half the size and sort of lost in a too-big rumpled tweed jacket.

Dad bear-hugged him, roaring laughing.

"Hey!" Luke punched him boisterously. He paid the driver and got his case from the boot. He saw us girls, standing awkwardly in pyjamas at the hall door. "Hi y'all! Your father licked ma ear!"

His accent was exotic – even more southern than Dad's.

"It's sure good to see y'all!" Laughing with happiness, Luke dragged his case up the path.

It was big.

How long was he staying?

Luke's hair stood on end like a character out of the Simpsons. Otherwise he was lithe with that healthy tanned American look, from vitamin D or something – they keep up with their vitamins in America. I'd tried to get Dad to take them, but he scoffed at the notion. Anyhow they probably wouldn't make any difference to your skin, Dad had been in Ireland long enough to be pasty-faced.

23

"Why didn't yuh call? I'd have come to meet yuh." He reverted to the soft southern tones of his youth. Dad had lived all over the south and the accent was a mixture, about as hard to describe as a smell or a taste.

"There was a line of cabs," Luke yelled.

Dad grabbed his case. "Yuh still shoulda called."

Call? With no phone? And meet him? Without a car? Dad was crackers. But their delight in each other intrigued me. I now knew what a buddy was. A buddy loved you.

Luke thumped Dad. "You're looking good, old son!"

"And you've still got hair!" he roared in despair. Hair was big with Dad. Then they started wrestling boyishly on the grass. Lucky we had high hedges.

Finally Luke called pax, and Dad gave up.

It was true about Luke's hair. He was hairy all over and carried a shopping bag. I discovered he was a cosy bookish person, the furthest point on earth from anything armyish. Something about him reminded me of Bilbo Baggins. You found yourself looking for furry feet.

That was later, really.

When Katie and I were introduced properly in the sitting room, Luke seemed taken aback. "Gee, Dan, your girls are grown!"

Katie and I shuffled awkwardly. What did he expect? Dad was old enough to be a grandfather. And Luke had four boys who were all still young – three were with one wife and one with another. He'd been married and divorced twice and had two current girlfriends.

"This is Clare?" Luke gaped at my sister.

Katie giggled idiotically.

I stepped forward. "She's Katie, I'm Clare."

People always thought my sister the elder.

24

"Hi, Clare. – Luke shook my hand solemnly. "Yuh outta high school yet?"

I nodded. "Just finished."

I was his height, but Katie towered over him. Maybe that's why, after they shook hands, he kept looking up at her in awe. I knew his thoughts exactly: "There's a pretty one and a plain one." A teacher in school had once described the Kelly sisters thus.

No wonder I had complexes.

Luke took books from his case. "I picked these up."

Anne of Green Gables and *Anne of Avonlea*.

Of course, we'd read them years ago, but it'd be rude to say so. Besides, it'd do Katie good to read them again. Luke was obviously a man of taste. They were the best books ever written – for children or not. Matthew and Marilla were my favourite characters in all of literature. For years, I'd imagined living with them on Prince Edward Island instead of with our own grandfather and grandaunt. I was Anne with freckles, red hair and a boyfriend called Gilbert. I cried and cried when Matthew died. Maybe they'd put Lucy Maud Montgomery on the Leaving – she was a dead white female.

"Thanks." I took mine.

He still couldn't take his eyes off Katie. "Hope y'all haven't read 'em?"

I nudged her. "She hasn't!"

"Eh – no!" Katie clutched her book happily. She was always delighted to get anything. She was like Heather in that. It was one of her good points. I suppose she had to have some. Everyone does.

Luke rooted in his case again. "I got candy for Heather and Bourbon for you, old buddy. It's still your drink?"

My heart stopped.

Dad shook his head. "Ah, no . . . I'm on the wagon."

Luke blinked unbelievingly. "That's a surprise."

"Had to, old son." Dad glanced nervously at the bottle, mockingly slitting his throat. "It was that, or else."

Luke looked worried.

"But you go ahead," Dad added quickly.

Luke put it back. "Eh – no . . . maybe later."

So we all had tea – there was no Nescafé. Then, while Dad cooked one of his disgusting abattoir breakfasts, they recalled *ad infinitum* old times and old friends. They'd met on their first day in the army which they'd both absolutely hated, dated girls together, and been shipped to Vietnam together.

"Whatja doing these days?" Luke asked, as sausages sizzled smokily.

The smoke alarm went off – it always did this, as there was no expel-air. Grandfather had a phobia about fire and gave it to us as a house-warming present.

As I fanned it with a newspaper, Dad opened the kitchen window, getting animated. "I'm in production."

Production?

What was he talking about? Did he mean that daft Shakespeare idea? I thought he'd forgotten that. That it had been safely shelved along with his other mad ideas.

But Luke was impressed.

I looked at Katie.

She, of course, never worried and gazed adoringly, as Dad related his plans.

"Yep. There's a need for more contemporary plays."

Would anyone go to them? And what'd he do for money?

"The Abbey's only interested in revivals," he said earnestly, "Shaw, Yeats, Synge, O'Casey, Friel. After that, forget it."

Luke was puzzled. "They don't do anyone new?"

Dad shook his head. "Hardly ever."

Maybe there was a reason?

After breakfast that morning Luke took his jetlag to the couch, while Dad went to his AA meeting, and Katie and I hung out in the dining-room and dreary kitchen, trying not to make noise, till Heather got home. It was awful, with Luke asleep we were afraid to even turn on the radio. With no TV, Katie and I were hooked on the radio – she on 98FM pop music, me on artistic BBC programmes. Heather was hooked on Gay Byrne, Pat Kenny and Marion Finucane, while Dad liked the news. He wouldn't let a TV in the house – according to him, it was absolutely ruining live theatre. Oh, he said that – really we couldn't afford one. The licence was £62. I was sorry we wouldn't be seeing Wimbledon. At Grandfather's I'd always got hooked.

That evening I waited for Heather outside the Bray book shop. We often did the shopping on her way home from work. I loved doing ordinary things with her – shopping, getting dinner. Other people would think me weird, I know. I'd phoned her about Luke, saying that we needed extras – orange juice and something for tomorrow's lunch.

At the Quinnsworth pizza counter I tackled her about Dad's production. "Dad's planning things again."

She blinked vaguely. "Planning what, darling?"

"He told Luke he was in production."

Heather giggled worriedly. "He didn't!"

"He did! He said there was a need for more modern plays."

She shrugged. "Perhaps he meant the play he was in."

"But he wasn't producing that."

She selected toppings for tomorrow's lunch – cheese and

olives. "No tomato sauce," she reminded the assistant. Katie didn't like it, so we all had to suffer.

I tried again. "He can't put on a play. He's on the dole."

Heather moved to the butter aisle.

"What about funding?" I persisted.

She frowned, picking up a tub of *Flora* margarine. "This the brand you like?"

I nodded. It was high in polyunsaturates. All the others were half water.

Resignedly I got milk. Heather didn't seem at all fazed by Dad's plans.

At the check-out I took the groceries out of the basket. "It might end up like everything else."

Heather looked curious. "How, darling?"

"A disaster."

She smiled. "Clare, you're worrying again."

That's all she ever said. But someone in the family had to worry. Usually me.

Chapter Three

Dad had cheered up since Luke came – only now he talked all the time about putting on plays. He was finally going to make it. This optimism was nearly worse than his previous despair and was getting to Katie. She was always out now.

I couldn't sleep till she got in.

One night the bedroom door creaked open.

"Who's there?" I whispered into the dark.

"Dracula, idiot!" ·

It was only her, coming in. My sister's weird in a lot of ways – clothes, music, grungey friends who want to rave to the grave. She'd been on the seafront with them. They were having another cider party, while I'd dozed over Roddy Doyle. I seemed to sleep all the time, while Katie just ran wild.

Had she been drinking tonight?

Or raving.

As she flicked on the light, I shielded my eyes. As usual she was wearing my new top – luckily my jeans were half-mast on her. Clothes were a thing we fought about.

"Who's there?" She mimicked me, undressing. "Who'd ya think it was?"

I didn't answer. She just hadn't *got it* that *Hamlet* opens like that.

"'Where does a goose come from?'" she jeered.

I said nothing.

"'A gooseberry bush!'"

I ignored her dig, not in the mood for a row. "It's after twelve."

She wriggled out of her jeans and into her sweat suit. Even in hottest summer, she went to bed dressed for a polar expedition. "So what?"

"So Dad said eleven-thirty."

"Get a life, Grandma!"

Her voice was thick.

"You've had cider!"

"So what!"

"So, what if I tell Dad?"

"Tittle-tattle!"

"Remember what happened to him?"

She looked upset, so I stopped. Our father was on the bottle for years. There was no harm in an almost sixteen-year-old sipping cider. I just worried about Es and stuff. And her hanging round with bad company. As I said, she'd been puffing behind hedges since age ten. They were all at it. You saw them all around Bray. I'd seen her with rough-looking boys in the Esplanade shelter. They were drinking bottles of water – which meant only one thing: Es. One of them had orange hair. Among her friends, Katie was the one piece that didn't fit. She just couldn't look grungey, no matter how hard she tried. Once she didn't comb her hair for a year, but still looked beautiful.

I was sorry now. "You might get hooked."

No answer.

"Then you couldn't quit."

Silence.

I tried again. "Addiction runs in families."

Still silence.

"What about River Phoenix?" I tried again. His poster was on her side of the room. Along with the Gallagher brothers, Jason McAteer and Gary Kelly. "He's dead."

No good.

She got into her side of the bed and thumbed violently through U Magazine. I didn't know what she saw in magazines. Plays were my hobby, especially collecting first lines. Shakespeare was still on my mind – because of Roddy Doyle. Were they really putting him on the Leaving? My school days were over. But Katie was another matter.

A pity to deprive her.

In Transition Year she'd dossed, but read for the first time – Stephen King and Maeve Binchy. A teacher told me all non-readers begin like that. At least it was a start. That's in between all the boys. Boys were her latest fad and cheaper than horses. Anyway they were bound to happen. Who'd she been with tonight? Tom, Dick, or Liam?

I knew all about sex from reading Edna O'Brien. But I wondered how far Katie went – what if she got HIV?

I asked once, but was told to mind my own business. She was sickeningly beautiful, actually. One of those gangly, carefree social successes. People stared after her in the street, which was hard on me. I was bookish and ordinary. Also a virgin.

Wally, my boyfriend, said I resembled a librarian. Maybe because of my new hornrims. Anyway, it was his last barb before departing for California. He was a BA in philosophy and got a job there clearing tables – you had to be well qualified. Oh, we were more friends than lovers, still his description hurt. A librarian? When I hoped to be a famous actor. He said I could play character parts. It wasn't fair, having a sister like Katie.

She still stared at the magazine.

I put on a nightshirt. "I'm turning out the light."

"I'm reading!"

"And I'm sleeping!"

"You're boring!"

She won, but the light kept me awake.

"What's up?" I finally relented – after all, her looks weren't *totally* her fault.

No answer.

Just more thumbing of pages.

"Oh, what is it?"

She flung her magazine down. "Why'd she DO it?"

I pretended ignorance. "Who's she? The cat's mother?"

"Heather, idiot!"

"Do what?"

"Get pregnant, idiot!"

Hmm. It was a good question and I didn't answer immediately.

"It was a mistake," I said at last.

Katie groaned.

"And she didn't DO it alone," I added.

My sister made a face. "Haven't they heard of contraception?"

I'd wondered the same. Actually I'd asked Heather, who told me she'd come off the pill for a month because she read you got cancer. Instead she got pregnant – it was the lottery of life. At first she thought she was putting on weight. "I'm sorry, Clare," she said when it was confirmed. "I won't leave things to you, I promise." I said it was about time she stopped saying sorry. Heather told me everything, but it wasn't right to share intimacies with Katie – she was too young.

"Or abortion!" my sister snapped.

"What about it?"

"Hasn't she heard of that either?"

I was philosophical. "That's a bit strong."

Abortion was on everyone's mind in Ireland. Along with divorce and that. People were either for it or against – either way it was on their minds.

"She's too old," Katie moaned from under the blanket.

"Not nowadays."

I got up to wash my teeth. Older women sometimes miscarried.

Dad's Clairol hair dye was in the dank shower room. Didn't he know it looked funny? I'd never dye my hair. Heather had lowlights and Katie highlights, which both looked natural. She was overreacting now, about the baby. So was I. Maybe it'd be OK. Health was Heather's latest kick. Thanks to me she ate properly and had got rid of her asthma with snake venom. And she'd never have an abortion. She believed in the life force, and had spent that very evening thinking of names for the baby. They'd considered calling it Mary after our President, whom Heather admired. Or after one of the Clintons – Dad liked Hillary and Heather thought Bill handsome, also he'd said there was a place called Hope. Finally they decided on Daniel or Danielle, after Dad. Who else?

I knew what was bugging Katie.

It wasn't really the baby. Like me, she was afraid Dad would leave. He'd lose money on a play and go back to London. He had once. And, despite Luke, he was getting more elated by the day.

I went back to bed. "Maybe they wanted another chance."

But no answer.

Katie was asleep.

I huddled at the edge of the bed, avoiding the canyon in

the middle. I never wanted children and if marriage meant sharing a bed, I had my doubts about that too.

Still, everyone deserved another chance.

Like we'd got now in Bray. With the sea for walks and the Head to climb it was like we'd died and gone to Heaven – except for Sellafield across the water. There was even a library for me and a swimming pool for Katie. She liked all sports, especially hockey. She'd wanted to live in a housing estate semi-d with three ceramic ducks flying over the mantelpiece – the more ordinary the better. She'd always wanted to do bourgeois things like invite her friends to tea, but we couldn't trouble Grandfather – older people fuss too much. Now Katie said our house was too dreary. It was old-fashioned and thirtyish, yet I liked it. Lately Heather'd even got domesticated. She'd bought cake tins and a gadget for boiling potatoes – it whistled at you when they were done. It boded well for our future of cakes and mashed potatoes. But the baby would leave no time for cooking.

Already she knitted non-stop. She was now on a matinée coat.

Pink.

So it must be a girl.

I wondered if she'd ever knitted for us. She kept saying she felt twenty-five again. But the Age of Petroleum wasn't a good one to be having a baby in. She'd forgotten Chernobyl and all those red tides, and whales dying like flies. And especially how boring babies were. How they woke in the night. Would it be a case of, "Hello baby, goodbye daddy?" It'd definitely be another excuse to leave. Or go back on the bottle. Alcoholics lived by the day.

But Dad wasn't drinking. And he might get a job. Dublin was the *in* place for actors. What with films like *My Left Foot* and *Into the West* and *The Commitments*, he was in the right place. He knew Jim Sheridan and Neil Jordan.

But I lay there, getting depressed.

The world was in decline – unemployment, global warming, the North Pole melting, the Black Sea poisoned, rave and house music clogging the airwaves, and all the junk on TV. And the Roddy Doyle controversy here. I mean, compare and contrast the following statements. "Good night, sweet prince" and "Eff off, bastard."

What'd a kid make of that?

There was a poverty in modern writers – too much effing and blinding. Imagine one starting with, "Attend, my Lord of Gloucester."

Finally I got to sleep on Lear's speech: "Blow winds, rage, crack your cheeks . . ."

It suited my mood.

Like all Americans, Luke was used to a lot. But nice. Although a bad diabetic, he never complained about the food. And he never drank in front of Dad, just secretly spiked his coffee. He was bright too – he saw pretty quickly that we were on our uppers.

There was the shabbiness of the house. Also Heather's spaghetti would convince anyone. Especially as we had it two nights running.

I'd got the wholemeal stuff and made a cheese sauce and a salad, which improved things.

He ate his plate of complex carbohydrates with relish, complimenting Heather on the sauce.

"This is great, Heather," he repeated the second night.

It was probably the only time anyone ever praised her cooking.

"Great!" he said again.

She reddened in delight. "Oh, Clare made that. I just boiled the spaghetti."

Luke munched enthusiastically. "Delicious."

I couldn't help smiling at the idea of deliciously boiled spaghetti.

Then Luke turned to me. "Yuh like cookin', Clare?"

I nodded – for some reason Luke made me shy. I felt he could read my thoughts and knew that I'd resented him.

"Why the brown pasta, darling?" Dad grumped at Heather.

"Sorry, Dan. Clare says it's healthier."

I nodded, my mouth full.

Dad chewed on, frowning. "For cows, Clare."

"It's buckwheat," I said. "The white stuff's full of toxins."

Dad was unconvinced. "This stuff's full of rubber." He looked at Luke. "Clare's worried that we'll get Mad Marrow Disease."

Everyone laughed.

I ignored them. I was afraid of meat. It thickened the blood and what if we went gaga? Life was hard enough without staggering.

"I'm sorry about the pasta, darling." Heather apologised again.

I wanted to strangle her.

Would she ever stop saying sorry? Brown pasta had more fibre. After all, you *are* what you eat. We were meant to be eating carbohydrates. And she should be having tofu for her age – except unluckily she wasn't menopausal yet. That was something to look forward to. Although I was getting more used to the idea of the baby. Both Katie and I were. My only dread was Grandfather's reaction.

I couldn't face him, so phoned to say I couldn't do the garden that week.

Grandfather was a misanthropist. There were enough human beings in the world, he always said. And the species was so flawed that God should crack the mould and begin again. He'd made a big mistake in creating us.

"We'll have steak tomorrow, darling!" Heather was saying.

"Great!" Dad grumped.

Luke just smiled at me. "I'll make y'all somethin'."

I hoped Dad was listening.

He was still grappling with the spaghetti.

Why didn't he cook dinner occasionally? He was well able to, and had a string of dishes from his southern youth: Chicken gumbo, fried chicken and hushpuppies, chicken-filled crêpes. He even knew some Indian chicken curry recipes from his job in a London restaurant. A wonder he didn't start flapping.

Then Luke announced, "I'm buyin' the groceries tomorrow."

Heather looked relieved, but Dad held up his hand. "Not necessary, old buddy."

What was he saying?

"No, I insist," Luke said. "While I'm visitin'."

"Wouldn't hear of it." Dad was firm.

I cleared my throat. "Eh – he could –"

"No!" Dad kept up his act.

Heather was red again. "Eh, Dan – ?"

"No, I'm expecting money."

"Money?" the three girls said together.

Dad looked defiant. "Eh – a grant. From the Arts Council."

We all looked at him.

He was getting dangerously worked-up. "For the play."

"What play?" I asked.

"I didn't know about that, Dan . . ." Heather's voice trailed off.

"The one I'm producing!" Dad banged the table exuberantly.

I looked at Heather.

Couldn't she stop him? I thought producing a play was just another whim, that he'd shelved it – especially now that he was unemployed. Like his idea of growing cranberries on the Bog of Allen, or growing Ramie in Florida – which was some fabric used in paper. Or his absolutely brilliant idea of importing pecans, so that the poor deprived Irish could feast on one million calorie pecan pies. But the play wasn't another whim. He was deadly serious.

"First, I thought of Shakespeare in the Green. Then – a modern comedy."

Luke lit a cigarette. He was suitably impressed and spoke through his usual plumes of smoke. "The Arts Council will fund it?"

Dad nodded. "Well . . . I'm applying. So there's no need to pay for groceries!

"You'll need that for production costs," Luke insisted. "Meantime, I can pay my way!"

Luke was one of those gentle, firm people. Once he said something, you didn't cross him. So it was settled: He'd help with expenses. Which solved all our food bills and was a great relief to me. There was still rent to pay. And now that we were putting on a play, there'd be other expenses.

Money was a problem.

It always was in our family.

But Dad was determined and desperate to go ahead. He went around now on a continual high, working out that we needed about three or four thousand pounds to rent a theatre, pay for publicity, and keep the actors going during rehearsal and the first week. By then there'd be box office money to pay them.

It sounded easy.

The Arts Council was supportive, but not enough to come up with anything. You had to fill out forms and be recommended and that. Also, as an American, Dad was suspect. In Ireland they'd know what you had for breakfast. Dad had never finished Trinity. And now was an unemployed actor with a reputation for drink. Years ago, he'd walked off the stage in the middle of a play. Then gone on a bender for a few days. And, like elephants, the Irish never forget. It's amazing they don't grow trunks while they're at it.

So things looked bad.

Also there was the question of finding an actual play to produce. One writer was willing and then withdrew. Dad talked on in his deluded way, with nothing definite in mind, which was just typical. You'd think with so many Irish writers around, he could find something quickly – a comedy, tragedy or history. But no.

I prayed he'd forget the whole thing.

Then Luke came to the rescue again. He liked theatre too, and, as well as being a professor, had actually dabbled with production and writing. He'd had plays staged in America. One evening after we'd walked the Bray Esplanade for our evening constitutional, and were having our bedtime cup of tea, he suddenly announced, "Hey, Dan . . . I've got a new play."

Dad looked eager. "You have?"

"Yes, a comedy I've been tinkering with."

"Well, let me read it."

Heather had the wit to look nervous.

Luke was delighted. "It's about a group of people putting on a play."

"Any sex in it?" Katie asked typically.

39

Dad gave her a stern look, but Luke just laughed. "There's a part for a sex fiend, OK."

My sister jumped up. "I'll play it!"

What was she talking about? *I* was the actor.

Luke's play was a farce called *Tennessee Tierney has not Lived in Vain.* About a rich businessman/politician who hires a writer, director, assistant stage manager and four actors to put on a play with a part for his out-of-work floozie – an ex-American movie actress, well past her use-by date, called Shirley Temple O'Shea. A sort of play-about-a-play with eight parts, *including one for me:*

In order of appearance they were:

Brad Hickey, a play director, about 35

T Boyle O'Reilly, a rich entrepreneur and politician

Art McCarthy, an actor about 25

Pembroke Parks, an actor about 70

Perdita Fitzpatrick, his wife, an actress about 78

Shirley Temple O'Shea, an American actress about 40

Tennessee Tierney, a playwright about 25

Penny Wise, a set designer about 25

I could be Penny Wise.

If only Dad would let me.

It'd be my big break. After that I'd have no trouble getting picked for the Samuel Beckett Centre in Trinity. I'd have experience of the professional Dublin stage.

I dropped hints.

But Dad said nothing about casting me.

He was on the constant high now about Luke's play, saying all the time that it was the very thing for the silly season. A sort of modern Dublin *Midsummer Night's Dream.*

With us putting it on, it was like a Chinese box. I mean, we were a group of people putting on a play, about people putting on a play. Would anyone come to it? I kept mentioning my doubts to Heather, and she kept saying not to worry. With Luke involved, I gave up and kept up my hopes about playing Penny Wise. After all, Dad had said anything's possible. At least his new mood was better than his previous state of depression. We had Luke to thank for that. I'd been crazy to resent him. Far from being the difficult guest, he brought sunlight into our dark little house. And much more was to be forgiven him, when he offered a thousand pounds for the production.

The only problem was the second thousand.

And the third.

And . . .

It didn't look good.

I got glummer and glummer.

Chapter Four

Luke had a phone installed first thing.

He needed to keep in touch with his family. As well as having four sons, two ex-wives, and two current US girlfriends, all on the best of terms, he found another red-headed girlfriend on arrival in Dublin. Between the lot of them, the phone never stopped ringing – sometimes it rang in the middle of the night.

They all asked his advice about the most petty things – cooking recipes, or how to fix the car, or change a fuse. Once someone rang from Virginia, asking how to spell a word. And his first wife wanted to know what was the name of the ship in *Moby Dick,* and Mimi's real name in *La Bohème.* She was doing a crossword puzzle.

Americans lived on the phone.

Dad did too.

He was always busy now – mostly fundraising. He was either meeting someone in the pub or phoning them elatedly. And in the evenings he sat in the kitchen, feverishly doing endless sums on a jotter.

Otherwise he and Luke talked non-stop about the play.

Well, almost non-stop.

Luke's fatal flaw was being a morning person. This was particularly noticeable on Sundays. He'd sit in the kitchen, while you were reading the papers, chain-smoking and talking his damn head off. Blab, blab, blab . . .

It was terrible.

"Anything interesting in the papers, Clare?" he'd ask.

I always shook my head.

He'd keep jabbering on, asking things like, "Any news from Bosnia, Clare?" Or "What are they doing in China?"

I'd look up in despair from the book review section.

But he wouldn't shut up. His blue eyes were always alert, his thick hair standing on end, behind a cloud of cigarette smoke.

"You have the news section," I'd remind him.

"Hmm . . . So I do!"

Then he'd rustle his newspaper, read a sentence aloud, wanting some sort of comment. Then smoke more, rustle more, read silently for another minute, and ask some more idiotic questions. Finally he'd make himself a Bloody Mary, and Virgin Marys for us. When Katie came in, he'd involve her in some inane conversation. Being divorced and girlless, he seemed to be curious about what we two thought – about everything: books, music, the Russians, the ozone hole, you name it. He was interested in everything and said he'd always wanted a daughter, so I suppose we were substitutes. It was vicarious fatherhood.

Apart from this, he was an ideal visitor.

As well as groceries and the phone, he got us real coffee and a real coffee percolator.

I like a proper cup of coffee.

In a proper, copper, coffee pot.

That was another tongue-twister from my acting class.

43

Would my exercises ever be any use? An acting teacher had told me that although my voice was light, I had a real stage presence.

But Dad never said anything about casting me.

Neither did Luke.

If he wasn't helping Dad, Luke left for the National Library to do his Boucicault research after breakfast on weekdays and came home late at night. Sometimes we walked the Esplanade then, where the fairy lights were lit for the summer. One night we saw a boy in soaking black shorts and T-shirt building a sandcastle. He was about twelve or thirteen with red hair and too old for buckets and spades. He looked like a French visitor, but I wasn't sure. He was frantically scooping up the sand into a pile, then the sea'd come in and he'd throw himself, spread-eagled, over it to stop it being washed away. He kept building and the tide kept coming in relentlessly. He tried so hard, but it was hopeless. We walked as far as the harbour and, on the way back, saw that the boy had given up. The castle was washed away and he was dressed.

Luke laughed. "A metaphor for life."

I thought of us: would our family survive? Or be washed away in a flood of bills? A play was a sort of sandcastle.

We always had a cup of tea before bed. At that time of night Luke was wonderful company. He talked endlessly then too, almost as much as Dad. He'd met Kevin Kline. He'd studied acting under Uta Hagen in New York and had hoped for a Hollywood film career. But he was only about five foot three and had flat duck-like feet and a sort of waddly walk.

I liked our evening chats. I was awake then and not deep in the Sunday papers. It was different, Luke being a lecturer and intellectual. I suppose, what I'm saying is: he took women seriously – Heather, Katie, and especially me. He told me all

44

about Shakespeare, Goldsmith, Sheridan, and Boucicault. And I lent him my Roddy Doyles – who, according to Luke, was a modern realist. I didn't know. He'd never be Shakespeare. Or Elizabeth Bowen or Lucy Maud Montgomery. And had he anything important to say? You had to make a statement – an English teacher told me.

Meantime, I job-hunted and Katie met her friends. Heather worked, while Dad was busy with the play.

It took all his time.

He hardly ever thought about anything else. Still it was good having him occupied and not fussing about dog dirt. Or the laundry. Or founding FANG, or HANG or MANG – depending on whether he was a father, husband or a mere man against nagging girls. He was happy now, working with Luke. They went out together a lot, meeting actors in pubs to discuss parts. And when they were at home, there was a lot of laughter.

One day I looked at theatres with them.

First we inspected an old cinema turned theatre in Pearse Street – the Academy – which Luke said was part of the Antient [sic] Concert Rooms where the Irish Literary Theatre first staged Yeats's *The Countess Cathleen*. He told me students from the university hissed – James Joyce was there, but didn't join the rioters. He'd used the theatre as a setting for one of his stories in *Dubliners*. I'm not a Joyce fan, but being in a building he'd known was fateful. Maybe it'd be lucky. Although there'd been a fire, the theatre was sort of upmarket in a seedy way. It wasn't any makeshift hole and I could imagine an audience coming. But Dad said it was too dear. So was every other theatre in Dublin.

Andrews Lane.

And the Project.

45

And even the Focus.

The next venue was a hall over a shop in Talbot Street, called the Pigsty. It was the home for a young theatre group – the Pig's Litter. It had a small stage and a dressing-room behind. The walls were peeling paint and there wasn't much space, backstage or front.

We couldn't be taking this?

Dad was eager. "Hmm . . . this'll do nicely."

Was he off his head? "Dad . . . ?"

"It's affordable, Clare."

Luke sniffed approvingly. He looked around, biting his upper lip. "A coat of paint'll work wonders, Clare."

So they took it. The mid-town position was good – there was parking and the overflow from the Abbey Theatre.

While Dad and Luke contacted more actors, I went into Dublin daily, job hunting. I didn't get anything, but loved walking around. I'd follow the people from O'Connell Bridge to College Green, then Grafton Street, and up to Stephen's Green where I'd watch the lovers and wonder if I'd ever be one. Where did all the people come from? The city was bustling with vendors, street artists, etc. The Diceman was gone now, and Pat Tierney who'd recite you a poem for a £1, but there was always some kind of music. And hardly a seat to be had in Bewleys – ever. I always went in for a coffee after trying about ten shops. The city was packed with the unemployed. And I was no exception.

Neither were actors.

You'd think it'd be easy to cast a play. Unemployed actors were crawling out of the woodwork in Dublin. At first nobody wanted to work for Dad. Everyone suspected an American. To their elephantine memories, Dad would always be the drunk who'd walked off the Gaiety stage in the middle of that play.

Yet other actors had walked off too – Daniel Day-Lewis in Hamlet. And more recently Stephen Fry had left a London play. Dad was a reformed character now, thanks to the Twelve Steps. He called up a few biggies who weren't working, but no luck. People were too suspicious of a play called, *Tennessee Tierney has not Lived in Vain.*

They finally cast some roles. The actors agreed to fifty pounds a week during rehearsal and a cut of the box office when we opened.

Eight multiplied by fifty equals four hundred and fifty pounds. That plus the theatre rent added up to more than we had. Luke had only invested a thousand. When I asked Dad where he was getting the rest of the money, he was vague. "Oh, a dab here, a dab there."

"Has anyone else invested?"

He raised his eyebrows. "A wangled teb, Clare."

"What if it fails?" After all it was a possibility.

"Then I get a proper job."

I couldn't believe it. "Nine to five?"

He crossed his heart. "Promise. This is my last turkey, Clare. Don't you worry."

So I didn't.

With Luke there, maybe I didn't have to.

Anyhow it was a good play. Very funny and sweet. The characters were all lovely. How could it fail? Still Luke was nervous, I could tell. He said Dublin's a city where only the past is revered. If we were putting on Yeats, Synge or Beckett, or anything sad or even rural, everybody'd flock to us. It might be different for a modern urban comedy.

I hoped he was wrong.

Finally I got a job in a hat shop in Stephen's Green Shopping Centre. In case I was called on to act, I religiously read plays aloud. And kept up my exercises: relaxation, breathing, and especially one for nasal resonance.

I regularly yawned on a low pitch.

Or recited at the bottom of the garden:

MUMMY, MUMMY, MUMMY, MUMMY, MUMMY, MUMMY, MUMMY, MUMMY.

Then MONEY x 8.

NINNY x 8

MEMORY x 8

REMEMBER THE MONEY x 8.

I worked on my monologue from *Dancing at Lughnasa*. If I was called for another audition, a new piece might impress them.

Dad held none.

He just took actors who looked right and were free.

One day our doorbell rang.

As no one ever called, I opened it cautiously – it must be someone collecting for something. Or someone wanting to clean the windows.

A boy resembling Andre Agassi stood outside with his bike. He had cycled all the way from Dublin and had an unshaven look, and a ponytail sticking out of a red baseball cap.

"Hi." I opened the door wider.

"I'm lookin' for Mr Kelly," he said. "I heard he's castin' a play. Does he live here?"

I nodded yes.

"Great!"

His accent was pure Dub. And his great smile.

I showed him into our dingy sitting-room.

He looked around. "Nice place ya got here – eh, what's yer name?"

"Clare. I'm his daughter."

"Hi, Clare. Shay Connors." He held out his hand.

I shook it. "A cup of tea?"

"Sure."

I got one.

While we waited for Dad, he told me he'd come to Bray as a chisler. It was a happy place for him. He did handstands on the beach and climbed the Head. That day he did handstands on our front grass.

I can't remember what else we talked about. Just that we did talk. Love's a kick in the stomach. That's all I can say. It gets you in the solar plexus and winds you completely. That smile knocked me back and the way he said, "Clare" – sort of flatly and rolling the r's.

When Dad came home, he gave Shay a scene to read. Then said he'd let him know.

I hoped it'd be yes.

It was. Dad cast him to play a young gay actor.

Finally all the parts were taken except the director, Brad Hickey, and Penny Wise, the ingénue set designer.

Please God, he wouldn't find anyone for her.

Then he might use me.

He'd talked to a few young women who weren't quite right. So my hopes rose. Why couldn't he pick me? I wasn't stunning like Katie, only OK looking. But I'd had some experience. I'd acted with a mask on my face. I'd even played the part of a banana. I could pant and bark like a dog.

My tactful hints were in vain.

Finally I asked outright, "What about *me*, Dad?"

He was sitting at the kitchen table, doing his calculations. "*You*, Clare?"

I tried to sound casual. "Yeah, I could do Penny Wise."

He sat there blinking.

"I could, Dad. I've acted all sorts of parts in acting school. Once I had a paper bag over my head."

His eyebrows went up.

"The audience had to guess what I was!"

He blinked. "Penny Wise is twenty-five, Clare."

"I can make myself older! I have a certificate in acting."

He shook his head. "No, you need an Equity card."

That wasn't true. I rang Equity, who said they'd give temporary cards if no suitable actor could be found. I was gearing myself to say this when he suddenly gave the part to Katie.

Katie? Katie!

It nearly killed me.

If I wasn't old enough, then she was nearly two years younger. And didn't even want the part. Besides she'd no experience. It was just her bloody brilliant looks. So much for feminism. Men were all the same. Life was a beauty competition. All our battles had been in vain, it still boiled down to how you looked, not what was between the ears. And sometimes I thought there was a large custard between hers.

I tackled Dad in the kitchen. "What about Equity?"

He was vague. "Hmm?"

"An Equity card. Remember you said a card was needed? Well, Katie hasn't got one either."

"Oh, we'll get around that."

I felt my face flame. "Couldn't you get round it for me?"

Dad frowned in puzzlement. "I need you for stage manager, Clare."

"Dad," I pleaded, "I'm the actress. Katie doesn't care."

"Katie has a wonderful – "

"What?"

"Eh – voice!"

I gaped. "Voice?"

"Yes, voice! Her voice is very good. I'm depending on you, Clare."

I couldn't look at him. "What's wrong with my voice?"

He didn't answer that. "You – you can be, eh, assistant director."

It sounded important, but my big break was gone. The one real chance of my whole life. "Katie's only sixteen."

He nodded. "She looks older. And she's seventeen in a month."

I slammed out of the room.

"Clare!"

"I have a job!"

I hid my misery among the midget raspberry canes at the end of the garden. Katie's voice was nothing special. But it was true about her looking old. Since age thirteen she'd looked about eighteen. Luke had even thought her the elder of us two. Still, I was sick with envy and disappointment. Absolutely green. Why did I have a beautiful sister? And probably another one on the way? It wasn't fair. Dad was rotten. Sexist. A definite male chauvinist. After all the years I'd stuck up for him with Grandfather. And all the times I'd heard him shout obscenities at Heather. When Katie always slept right through.

He followed me out to the garden, looking upset. "Please, pumpkin."

I didn't answer.

"I need you, Clare."

After a while I said, "What about my job in the hat shop?"

"I was hoping you'd give that up."

"I don't know if I can." It was a lie.

51

"They'll easily find someone else," he reasoned.

"But Katie's never had any acting lessons."

He said nothing for a second. "Acting's like swimming. You get lessons. Or you swim."

I was stunned.

"You jump in the deep end. Learn by doing."

After all my efforts to improve myself by memorising play first lines. By ooh-ing and m-m-m-ing and ah-ah-ing in empty rooms to train my voice. What about my deep breathing? And all my studying of the organs of articulation? How many people knew where their soft palate was? Katie didn't even know she had one.

"I need a stage manager – I mean, assistant director, Clare. You'll learn a lot."

I couldn't say anything.

"Will you give up the hat shop?"

I still couldn't speak.

"Please, Clare. I'm depending on you."

"OK."

What else could I say?

People depended on me. It'd always been the same – Grandfather, Heather, then I was head girl in school. Was it my librarian looks? I was small, plain and responsible, with big glasses. I was not Prince Hamlet, nor was meant to be. I was a spear-carrier. A stand-in. An extra face in a crowd. Oh, nobility's fine in a poem, but reality's another matter.

They also serve who only stand and wilt.

52

Chapter Five

I felt guilty about Grandfather's garden. Saturdays were for that.

Since moving to Bray, I'd gone back to help him and Aunt Brigid who were both absolutely ancient. They had a daily lady for indoors, who never cleaned and served the same greasy food every day – revolting frozen fish. Or mad cow pies. Yet Grandfather never complained, just ate everything gratefully. He could afford his daily, but depended on me for the garden. Gardeners cost a fortune. One had charged forty pounds to cut a miserable hedge. But Grandfather was too old to get up a ladder and his back too bad for weeding.

"What about hitting up the Ayatollah, Clare?" Dad said at breakfast one Saturday.

This was one of his names for Grandfather.

I was puzzled. "What do you mean?"

"Ask him to invest in the play."

"Oh." I was taken aback.

Heather's knitting needles stopped clacking. She looked up thoughtfully. "He'd do anything for you, Clare."

Heather always said this, but it wasn't true. Katie was the pet.

Amazing, as she refused to help with the garden – it was too boring, she said. More likely, she was too lazy.

"When we win the Lotto, we'll hire him a gardener," Heather said. Fantasising about winning was a regular habit of hers. The family was getting a new house. Dad a theatre. Katie a TV, and me a pair of rollerblades – it looked like great fun.

I hoped Dad would forget his daft idea.

But as I left, he yelled after me, "Mention the play, Clare!" I stood in the hall doorway.

"We need more investors," he added worriedly.

"He won't, Dad."

Dad still looked hopeful. "Tell him it could make money."

I was dubious. "But Grandad doesn't like anything modern."

"True." Dad frowned. "Hmm. Well, make sure he doesn't drive you to the train! I don't want you in hospital."

Dad never stopped about Grandfather's driving.

"He's not that bad," I said.

"He's terrible. His car should be confiscated."

All the way to the DART, I thought about how they rubbed each other the wrong way. Dad gave out about Grandfather's driving, but Grandfather didn't trust Dad either. He never had and never would. He didn't like wild colonial boys and that was that. Heather was his only daughter. And Dad didn't realise that someone from Tallahassee was an unsuitable son-in-law. Especially an out-of-work, dippie-hippie actor type, who was an ex-drunk and ex-wife batterer. Grandfather probably wanted a banker. Someone whose father was in school with him. Or a Rathgar type – maybe in Foreign Affairs, a striped-suited, stuffed-shirt who played tennis at Fitzwilliam. It'd be even better if he read *The Financial Times* and could advise about investments.

Instead Heather'd run away with Dad – pregnant with me.

They had wild student years.

Then unhappy Dublin years.

Then London.

A train was in the station. I found my usual window seat, facing the engine on the sea side. The DART was one of the reasons I loved Bray. You can read the poems inside, or look at the sea. Killiney Bay was the best view in Europe, according to G B Shaw and I certainly agreed. It was magic with sun on the water.

Grandfather's earliest memory was of sitting on the beach and hearing that the First World War had started. It was the happiest day of his life. And the world's last summer, like this was mine. It seemed unfair to be happy only once in all your life. He said life passed as quickly as a swallow flying through a banquet hall. He told me all about olden times when the railway was first built and only rich people lived in Killiney. The Vico Road had been closed to ordinary people then. He was a born story-teller. When we first went to live with him, Katie was small. She missed Heather and had temper tantrums, yet he never got mad. He just read her stories. I can still hear his old voice: "In a hole in the ground there lived a Hobbit."

Maybe he wanted a second chance too.

He'd failed so badly with Heather.

I was a sort of go-between. Their relationship had always been terrible. It wasn't fair. He gave out when she was in London for all those years. Yet now that she was home, he didn't seem glad at all. You can never please some people.

But Dad was cracked – he'd never invest.

Firstly our grandfather was irked that we girls had left him. For years he'd grumbled about *having* to have us. And now we'd deserted him, after all he'd done for us, blah, blah, blah.

He grumbled no matter what.

Secondly there was the matter of France – he badly wanted me to go and offered the fare again. But I wouldn't. And there was a third reason he wouldn't help – meanness. Sure, he wouldn't even let anyone vacuum the carpet in case it wore out the pile.

What was he saving it for? He already had piles, and not only of money.

Anyway, he didn't like modern plays, period. He only liked dead writers – Yeats or Shakespeare. Everything else was rubbish.

His house was yellowish Victorian brick, mellow in the afternoon sun. There was a lovely old-world garden. That day a late clematis bloomed by the drawing-room window. And there were red peony roses at the edge of the mossy lawn. Heather'd grown up there, so it had all sorts of memories. Although she said she hated it, my theory is that people leave an aura in a place after they leave it. For me the house was a part of Heather that she didn't want to recognise.

I pushed the squeaky gate, planning to take some cuttings for Bray – geranium and busy lizzy. The grass where Katie'd grazed a Traveller's pony had grown back – the heedless hoof marks were gone. Grandfather'd been mad that day, but she'd just shrugged, "It was hungry, what could I do?" And she got away with it. She always did. Oh, we had a happy life there, and a room each. But I missed the garden.

The geriatric dogs, Yuppie and Princess, came yapping down the path. One was a King Charles and the other a mad mongrel. Both were as arthritic as their owners.

As I patted them, Aunt Brigid appeared on the path from

the back garden. "Prenez garde aux chiens! Ah, ma petite, Clare."

Our aunt's one accomplishment in life was French – a sort of phrase book type unlike anything I'd heard there. She was petite, with pink, wrinkled skin and the remains of blonde beauty. She used to remind me of the Duchess of Kent at Wimbledon, although not so much these days. They were the same type – a blonde bun and sort of, I don't know, dressy. Hard to describe some people without sounding snobby, but Aunt Brigid's main occupation was shopping. She was a Brown Thomas type and had lunch there every Saturday, for as long as I'd known her.

"Hi, Brigid."

Although in her seventies, she still insisted on us calling her Brigid – "Aunt" was too geriatric. Crazy, but that was Aunt Brigid. She'd never done housework, and used to keep fit by gardening. These days she sort of flitted around with a dainty basket. That day, she carried one with cut flowers and shrubs and was dressed in Wellingtons and an old coat and straw sunhat hid her white-blonde hair.

I let her hug me.

"Ma petite."

She was always hugging people. Once she hugged the milkman who immediately dropped all his bottles. There was glass everywhere and rivers of milk flowed.

"You've got a bit of colour, Clare. It's all that lovely Bray air. C'est jolie au bord de la mer."

"Yeah, it's jolly nice OK."

"Jolie! Jolie! Naturellement, you do." Then she asked about my exams.

I said they went OK – I was trying hard not to think about points or places. Or being recalled for interview.

"How's Katie?"

"Fine."

"And Heather?"

I said nothing.

Aunt Brigid took my hand conspiratorially. "Now, Clare, Heather hinted at . . . ah . . . ?"

I played dumb. "Hinted at what?"

"Un bébé," she whispered, eyes wrinkling into a smile.

So she knew.

I hid my lack of enthusiasm. "Yeah . . . Eh, does Grandad know?"

She shook her head. We both knew what his reaction would be. He was negative about everything, so would hardly welcome a new baby. You learnt not to tell him anything. He was constantly griping – about the weeds in the lawn, the hedges, the state of the world.

"Let's not mention it," I said.

Aunt Brigid held a finger to her lips. "Sshsh!"

Grandfather loved small children – other people's. He'd think Heather's nothing but trouble – like Katie and me. I could just hear him, "I'm too old for anymore responsibility, etc., etc., etc." As if everyone wanted him to take on more. And Heather was going to leave the bassinet in Ranelagh.

I left Aunt Brigid dead-heading geraniums and went into the dark kitchen.

It had an big unused range and a well-worn quarry-tiled floor. The house was getting shabby. The upholstery and carpets were frayed. And the big old, brown furniture, once highly polished, was dull and dusty. There used to be a place for everything, etc. Now the glasses were greasy and there was grime everywhere. Grandfather's daily lady took money for nothing.

The lean-to conservatory was off the dining-room, overlooking the back garden. Grandfather was watering plants there. He was stooped a bit from arthritis. He wore his usual old cardigan and a straw hat to protect his bald head. "Hmm, it's you, Clare."

"How's your back?" I asked.

I always asked this.

As usual, he grunted. He had blue eyes and looked like a severe Alec Guinness, until he smiled – which was usually for Katie alone. Then he looked like a kind old man.

"You're looking well," I said as usual too.

He put down his can, and straightened his back painfully. "There are three ages in life – you're young, you're middle-aged and you're looking well."

I smiled – he always said this.

I loved Grandfather, although he was often a long drink of misery. And lately repeated himself all the time. Still, I did think he was looking well – for his age, which is about 157, well, not really. He just looked it sometimes. He went on watering, while I chatted, finally asking what needed doing.

"The dandelions are up again in the back," he grumped.

"Not for long. Demolition's my speciality!

He was puzzled. "You're debilitated and need a specialist?"

"No, I'm –"

"You said you were debilitated."

I reddened. "I said *demolition was my speciality*!"

"You should speak up, Clare. Open your mouth."

"Ahhhhh!" I opened my mouth a hand's width. We did it in acting class.

He blocked his ears. "There's no need to shout!"

You can't win. I got a hoe from the garden shed, passing the engraved stone plaque:

> The touch of the sun for pardon,
> The song of the birds for mirth,
> You're nearer God's heart in a garden,
> Than anywhere else on earth.

Heather had got it for his eightieth birthday. Why was there never any pardon for her? Grandfather was meant to have heart trouble. He certainly had it where she was concerned. Would they never get on?

The garden was full of trees – birch, ash – willow and it had roses and camellia bushes. It needed a lot of work and I'd promised Grandfather to get it right that summer. A weed was a flower in the wrong place. What did he have against dandelions? He had a fit when I served them once in a salad with nasturtiums. I worked for a couple of hours, uprooting weeds individually as grandfather hated weedkiller. Last year I'd made daisy stripes in the grass with it, which had upset him – caring about the environment's grandfather's one good point and the very opposite to Dad who doesn't even believe in global warming. He said it was all rot. A conspiracy. When I warned him the seas would rise, he'd just snapped, "We'll build a raft, Clare."

Gardening's OK when you get into it. It's satisfying tidying things up. And it lasts, unlike housework which needs to be redone the following day. Especially with Katie around.

"Le thé, Clare!" Aunt Brigid called me at last.

I washed my hands.

We always had tea in the conservatory – on the dot of half-four. There were cakes and Grandfather's homemade rock scones (brown for me) and jam – two kinds. Cooking was always his hobby. He used to do jam and cakes, but now he could only manage scones. Aunt Brigid wouldn't cook. She was used to maids all her life, as well as their ghastly daily lady now. Or else Grandfather did it. Anyway, cooking was better for his arthritis than gardening.

We were on our second cup when he asked casually, "Well, Clare, changed your mind about France?"

My mouth was full. "No, eh – thanks anyway."

He sniffed. "You'll regret it."

I said nothing.

"For the rest of your life."

He was always so doomy.

"She has her whole life to go!" Aunt Brigid butted in. "Elle est très jeune!"

"The time to learn languages is when you're young," he repeated for the millionth time.

"I'm glad we'll be seeing a bit of you, ma petite." Aunt Brigid was bubbly. "I'll teach you French."

"Merci."

I could imagine the type of French – miscellaneous expressions, polite expressions, expressions for cafés, and ones for buying railway tickets – before the war, the first war.

"We pass this way but once," Grandfather intoned. "Young people don't realise that."

Hell, it was the very thing I *did* realise. This was my first summer since age ten with parents in residence – even if one was pregnant.

He frowned. "What's keeping you here?"

"Dad's putting on a play."

"A what?" He spluttered apoplectically.

It'd just come out. Anyway, I wanted to get off France. I couldn't explain about us being a family again. How I wanted to experience it, if only for a summer, one summer before I was grown up completely.

"He's putting on a *what?*" Grandfather was recovering his breath.

"A play," I repeated. "P-L-A-Y. With actors."

Aunt Brigid got two red spots in the middle of her cheeks – a sign she was pleased. "Est-ce possible?"

I nodded. "Oui. For the summer."

Grandfather glared. "Where?"

"In a theatre. We're renting one. Hiring real actors and that. I was hoping for a part."

This threw Grandfather.

"But Katie got it. I'm stage manager."

"You're still determined on acting?"

"Yeah."

He gritted his teeth. "Well, be prepared for unemployment."

I said nothing. I knew exactly what he was thinking. That he'd paid out good money for Mount Prospect. Now he wanted me to do Business Studies and get a secure job with a pension like he had. A bank or a building society. He didn't realise that the world had changed and now people had floating careers. Mine would float into the theatre.

"It's insanity," he predicted now. "Your father's corrupted you. And now he's doing the same to Katie."

"Alex!" Aunt Brigid looked shocked.

Grandfather was staring dismally out the window. "What's the play?"

"It's new – Luke, Dad's American friend, wrote it. He came for the summer and they agreed a production."

"Agreed *on* a production!" Grandfather snapped.

"Agreed on . . . " I paused. "He's investing a thousand pounds."

Grandfather said nothing.

I knew he wouldn't be interested. He was too negative. The whole world was going to pot, according to him. No one even spoke the "King's English" properly anymore. I always asked him which King? Was it Henry VIII? Hadn't he noticed there was a Queen on the English throne? He always ignored me and grumbled that people said, "met with," when they meant "met." And even *The Irish Times* used words like "situation," when they meant "position." He could hardly understand anyone anymore and felt a stranger in his own country.

Grandfather laughed shortly. "Americans!" He spat out the word. "Hmm . . . he must be well-off, if he can throw away that much."

We fell into another munchy silence. Which Grandfather broke, "No one goes to theatre in the summer."

I thought for a minute. "Well . . . schools are on holidays."

He snorted.

"The schools! Formidable! Formidable!" Aunt Brigid kept burbling between mouthfuls of scone. Her blue eyes were bright, and she wriggled on her chair with excitement. "C'est épatant!"

I was puzzled. "Eh, what?"

"C'est épatant!"

"Oui," I muttered, not understanding.

Grandfather silently buttered another scone. After a few bites he said sarcastically, "Can't your father get a job like everyone else?"

"There aren't any," I said.

Grandfather grimaced. "Does he look?"

"He's creating his own."

"Creating his Waterloo!"

"It'll be work for others too." Then I blurted, "He was hoping you'd invest."

"What?" He started coughing. Almost choked.

I waited while he recovered.

"Well, I won't! Nor pick up the pieces afterwards. You can tell him that!"

It was no use arguing.

Grandad was now quite irked. "He never offered me a penny all the years you girls lived here."

I'd heard all that before. He was like a gramophone record stuck in a groove. "I know, Grandad."

"Not a penny!"

I listened patiently.

"A play indeed!"

Grandfather wanted to bring back hanging and shoot all the poor people. And he didn't believe in the arts, so how would he invest in a play? Dad was cracked. Lately Grandad couldn't even follow the most simple things on TV. He said there were too many characters and all the women looked the same. They should have introductory sessions for people like him. Like a list of characters – JOHN, A FARMER; MARY, HIS WIFE; TOM, THEIR SON.

Then he softened, shaking his head. "No, I'm afraid not. Not this time, Clare."

"Mais c'est épatant!" Aunt Brigid clasped her hands together.

What was she saying?

"If he needs help," she went on urgently. "I'm here. I have a small savings account."

This freaked Grandfather. "NO!"

"Alex!"

"You're not touching that!" He had charge of her money.

"I certainly am!"

64

"You're certainly not!"

She was hot and bothered and sat there working herself up into a state. "You've bullied me all my life!"

He stared stonily into space.

God, were they having another row?

"Tyrant!"

Her cheeks were blotched and an angry red line moved upward from her neck.

"Aunt Brigid . . ." I tried to soothe her, but it was no use.

Grandfather closed his eyes as she ranted on about how he had ruined her life. She still hoped to meet someone who'd take her away from her awful fate with grandfather. Once she disturbed a burglar, yelling, "Au secours! Au voleur!" He just gaped, so she asked him if he wanted to rape her. He was so shocked he fled. I told her later how stupid it was to provoke him. It wasn't funny at all. "I just wanted to save you two girls," she tearfully explained. But I think she was sorry he ran away.

Grandad took care of her – that's the truth.

She'd always had periods of madness. She imagined things, like people were following her. Or TV personalities were sending her messages because they loved her. Especially the actor who played McCall in *The Equaliser*. Also John Thaw in *Morse*. And Pat Kenny. Also Oprah Winfrey. But I could've kissed her now for offering to help Dad. All my relatives weren't philistines.

At last Aunt Brigid calmed down.

It usually took about ten minutes.

"Dad'll be glad of your help," I humoured her. "It doesn't have to be money. You can, eh – sell tickets. There'll be loads to do."

She clutched me eagerly. "Clare, ma petite! I've had acting experience."

Grandfather groaned. "Not another one."

"Tais-toi, Alex!"

Was this round two?

"What did you act in, Aunt Brigid?" I asked gently.

"I was Our Lady." She looked emphatically at Grandfather. "And your grandfather was the Angel Gabriel!"

He smiled sourly. "I've no memory of that."

"Don't you remember, Mother made you wings?"

He stood up and irritably stacked the tray.

"Out of her wedding dress?"

"No!"

"Oh . . ." Aunt Brigid looked so disappointed. "But we acted in a hall in Rathmines. I can remember staring out at the audience in my beautiful blue dress. I loved acting. It's one of my regrets that I didn't keep it up."

Aunt Brigid said this a lot. Life had been a big disappointment to her. She wanted to be famous for something. During Wimbledon, she regretted giving up her tennis. Or she could've been a famous pianist if only she had practised more and could play the piano better. Or a singer, if only she'd got the proper training. Now she wanted to be in on the play. She always wanted to be in on everything. Dad would find something for her to do. I'd make him.

Chapter Six

Instead of *acting* an assistant stage manager, I *was* one.

Maybe it was just reality. My lot was to be on the sidelines, to take care of things. To be a drone instead of the queen. Dad kept assuring me that a good ASM was vital to a successful production. And, since all our money was on this turkey, it had to fly.

I threw myself into my new job.

I photostatted the play, and the company met for the first time to read it. The Pigsty wasn't free yet, so for the first week we rented a rehearsal room at the top of one of the last crumbling Georgian houses on the Liffey quays. All around us were posh new apartments and shops. Our grotty room had a mushroomy smell. And no heat. But it was summertime, and heat didn't matter. Outside the river flowed inexorably. And inside there was a secondhand book and coffee shop on the first floor, which added a bohemian atmosphere and a sense of camaraderie.

I was still ill with envy of Katie, but hid it.

I was a Martha and always would be. Katie had the better part and it would not be taken away from her. At least I had some role to play. I was to read the stage directions that first day the cast met.

Unfortunately I'd told Aunt Brigid when and where we were meeting. She was waiting for us on the steps.

I was dismayed. She looked so frail and old. "Brigid."

"Ma petite." She kissed me.

"What're you doing here?"

She was all dressed up in her best ecru linen suit and matching straw hat. She waved her stick in puzzlement at the old house. "Est-ce le théâtre?"

"No, it's just a room – for rehearsal." I'd said she could help, but meant selling tickets or coffee once the play *started* for real.

Dad didn't look too happy either and made a face behind her back, indicating she wasn't welcome. *Get rid of her*, he mouthed at me, making a vamoose sign with his hand.

I nodded, turning to Aunt Brigid, "Eh – you're not needed today, Brigid."

She looked outraged. "Clare, I've come in especially."

I felt stabbed.

"All the way from Ranelagh," she pleaded.

"Not today, Brigid. There'll be lots to do later."

"Can't I hear the play?" Her old voice broke.

I was firm. "No, it's up three flights of stairs."

"I can manage the stairs."

"No. Eh – Dad's afraid it'll put the actors off," I said desperately.

"Oh . . ." Her face crumpled. "Well, I wouldn't like to do that." She sighed heavily. "I suppose I'll have to go home."

"You'll get the 11 bus?"

She nodded.

"Want me to walk you to the corner?"

"No!"

"Well, take care crossing the road."

I watched her hobble off, feeling so bad that I almost ran

68

after her. But I didn't. Dad was right. She'd only be interrupting, yelling things out in French. Bossing everyone around. Scaring the actors off.

When they had all assembled, except for one, Dad stood on a sort of platform. He introduced Luke, the playwright, as his life-long friend, and a distinguished academic who was writing an important book on the famous Irish playwright, Boucicault.

The actors were scattered about the room.

"Hi, guys." Luke stood up. "Glad to meet y'all."

They mumbled hello back.

Luke looked very American in his uniform Levis and Docksiders and brushing back his unruly, straight-up Simpson-like hair. He referred flatteringly to Dad's career in London. Then explained the play. "What we have here is a farce for the silly season, a send-up of the artistic life. It also has some touching characters – well, I think so."

People laughed.

"It should be played for laughs," he went on.

Everyone listened attentively.

I can still see them.

Katie in new leggings and, of course, my denim jacket, sat cross-legged on the floor. Looking terrific, as usual, with her thick blonde hair cut in a fringe at the front and tied in a ponytail behind. Naturally, she was positioned strategically between the two younger men – one was Jerry, a country type with a helmet of black hair and a Liam Gallagher look-a-like, playing Tennessee Tierney, the hick playwright; the other Shay, the Dub who had called out to our Bray bungalow that day. He'd got the part of Art, the proletarian actor. Jerry was potato-faced and a bit culchie, while Shay was handsomely punk. He now wore the same baseball cap back to front, and still had that permanently unshaven Agassi look, and two earrings in one ear.

69

Which one would Katie pick?

I prayed she'd like Jerry. Then I might get second choice. With Wally away, I definitely had a vacancy for a lover. But would Shay even look at me with my sister around? By flanking her that first day, both boys were obviously staking their claim to the honeypot.

Next were the two older actors playing the parts of the two Shakespearean actors. The woman was Ivy Biscovicz, a Countess in real life, who'd had a brilliant career in The Gate of all places; while the man was Angus Raftery, an experienced amateur actor from a theatre group in Bray. He had wrinkly skin, thick white hair super-glued over a bald patch and droopy wrinkled eyelids.

Beside them was Oliver Riley, portly and redfaced, a seasoned actor and redundant singing star of TV sitcoms. He looked like a serious drinker. He was to play the corrupt T Boyle O'Malley, the wealthy Irish entrepreneur, who was putting up the money for the play within the play – pity we hadn't someone wealthy in real life.

Last of all there was Bentley St Denis, an English public school type, who'd been finally found for Brad Hickey, the gay director in love with Shay's character, Art.

Only Fidelma Foley still hadn't come. She was the Irish actress picked for the American floozie.

We waited, but she didn't show.

Finally Dad held up his hand for silence. "I think we'll have to go on. We'll do a cold read now, so you can each get acquainted with your part. I'll read Fidelma's."

Bentley St Denis stood up pompously. "Excuse me, I can't do that."

Everyone looked awkward.

Bentley started making trouble from the beginning. Like he

wanted to be the real director or something, instead of acting the part in the play. I suppose the main impression he gave was of posh but unkempt shabbiness. He spoke a sort of lispish RP and acted like some sort of mogul. He was always talking on his mobile phone about "gigs" – even our play was a "gig." He had a long greasy ponytail and round wire glasses, such as John Lennon used to wear. His shirt hung out, and his running shoes were down at heel and dirty. Also he had BO and bad breath. How had Dad cast him?

Dad was genial. "What's the problem, Bentley?"

"I don't know what this character's thinking!"

"He's not thinking anything."

"Oh, come now!" Bentley griped.

Dad rustled his script. "He just wants to get on with it."

There was an awkward silence.

"I feel we should *ease* into our parts privately, more gradually." Bentley moved his hands as if he were directing a piece of pianissimo music. "Gently."

Dad tried to say something. "But –"

"Live with them a bit, get to know them." Bentley wouldn't let him get a word in.

"I –"

"*Feel* their pain."

From that first day Bentley was hooked on The Method. Didn't he realise he was only acting a part?

Dad concealed a smile. "Their pain?"

"Yes. Research their backgrounds."

Dad kept cool. "Oh, I think we'll just read it for now. We can research later."

Bentley banged his script at his side. "Sorry, can't do it."

There was another silence.

Dad was irked – I knew by the way he bit his upper lip.

Bentley looked as if he'd walk out. Everyone else looked embarrassed.

Then redfaced Oliver Riley closed his eyes and sang, "I Dreamt that I dwelt in Marble halls . . ."

He had a beautiful tenor voice.

"With vassals and serfs at my side . . ."

Everyone smiled.

Even Dad. "Thanks, Oliver."

The tension was gone.

Not for long.

Angus, the old man playing Ivy's husband, cleared his throat and said to Bentley in an exaggerated West Brit accent, "Forgive me, dear boy, but we're actors."

"That's just it!" Bentley seemed taken aback that someone was arguing with him. "That's just it!"

"Dear boy —"

"Actors act," Ivy added politely, fixing a stray strand of white hair under her wide straw hat. Her dress was a delicate powder blue and gave a weird air of youthfulness to her decrepitude.

"They don't *feel!*" Angus added.

"Where've you been?" Bentley snapped.

The older man was taken aback. "*Been,* dear boy?"

"You don't *feel!*" Bentley mimicked the old man. "That's old hat!"

"Old hats wear well!" Angus looked triumphant.

Dad smiled openly now.

I knew he liked the old people, especially the woman who was now almost forgotten in Dublin. The old man, as I said, was an amateur and had never been in a professional production before. They were typecast really, because except for being unmarried in reality, they seemed to be playing the same parts now as they had in life – the woman was the famous one. Also a little more frail. I had seen her climbing the stairs wearily on the way into rehearsal that day, then straighten up and quicken her step when she saw me.

"Yeah . . . buh we hafta feel it too," Shay said, rubbing his ear-ring. "Don't we, Mister Kelly?"

"It's Dan, Shay."

"Eh, Dan, then. Don't we feel too?"

"The play's a lighthearted summer piece," Dad repeated. "No one need worry about method acting. That's for the New York Stanislavski types. Oh, it has its place in theatre history, but it's dated now."

Shay was puzzled. "We're not to feel antin' then?"

Dad was patient. "The best way to approach a character is physically, rather than intellectually."

"Right oh, Dan." Shay gave the thumb-up sign. "Gottcha!"

"If you remember Cyril Cusack," he went on, "he always had some gesture, which got the character."

"Yeah! Gotcha! Gotcha!" Shay pored studiously over the script.

I was proud of Dad knowing so much. He was a brilliant director and a marvellous actor.

Shay's accent would curdle cream. He was right out of Roddy Doyle, a genuine Dub with a fondness for its most famous fricative. He said the F-word A LOT. Later I learned that his family lived in a flat in Rialto and, except for his ma, didn't approve of him going on the stage. They thought the dole was more respectable. He'd had some experience in the Project, but it was an uphill task convincing his da to let him act. I'm sure that's why Dad gave him the part. He's like that – up for the underdog. He knows what it's like, being one so often himself.

Dad called for silence now.

There was an expectant hush.

"OK . . . Let's take it from the top! Clare, you start with the stage directions."

I began nervously:

ACT ONE

The front curtains open partly, not entirely, on the undressed stage of a theatre in Dublin. It is morning and rehearsals are about to begin. A couple of tables and some small chairs are scattered about. The play director, Brad Hickey, comes on-stage, looks at the curtains, then goes back off and draws them the rest of the way. Then he puts some lights on. He looks about gloomily. He is a slight, vital little man of about thirty-five, dressed in sandals, extra tight jeans, a T-shirt, and a huge sombrero. His spectacles are suspended from a chain about his neck. He takes a script from his shoulderbag, holds it out distastefully, and drops it.

Bentley was meant to start, but stared sullenly at the script.

"Bentley?" Dad prompted. "Your cue."

"What?"

"Hickey's on!"

Bentley grunted. Then began, with me interweaving the stage directions:

Hickey:	What a script. No bounce!
I read:	*[He kicks the script.]*
Hickey:	That's the only way I'll get a kick out of directing you!
Me:	*[He takes out a vial and swallows two –]*

Before I had finished Bentley jumped in:

Hickey:	*Tennessee Tierney Has Not Lived in Vain*, what

74

a title! By Tennessee Tierney, what a name!
I'm to kick you into shape, eh. Well, take that!

Me: [*He kicks the –*]
Hickey: And that!

Bentley stopped abruptly, glaring at me, then Dad. "I pwotest!
I utterly pwotest!"

Funnily he had a lisp in real life, but not in the play.

Dad's mouth twitched. "What is it now?"

Bentley pointed to me. "She's reading too slow!"

My face went on fire.

He was stepping on my lines. I hadn't had a chance to read
the last words – *pills* or *script*.

"Clare!" Dad said gently. "Try and be quicker."

I nodded.

Dad was stupid. Couldn't he hear? Obviously not.

"OK," Dad said patiently, "take it from the top!"

We began again. The very same thing happened.

"I can't tolewate this!" Bentley yelled, stopping dead.

Everyone stared.

I prayed for the ground to open.

Then Luke stepped in. "There are too many stage
directions, Dan. It's holding things up. Clare, just read the
directions between the character's entrances. OK?"

I nodded nervously.

He squeezed my arm. "You're doing fine."

Thank God for Luke.

Dad sighed. "From the top!"

Bentley read the speech on his own. His character was
lamenting having to direct at all. He seemed an unpleasant
ham and just like Bentley:

75

What did T Boyle O'Malley say? "Just needs a bit of spit and polish." Well, try that for starters.

Bentley actually spat on Luke's script. Was it necessary? He continued vehemently:

Oh, ye gods, a man of my taste and experience, five years at the Bury St Edmund's Old Vic! Ye Gods, to descend to this – Tennesse Tierney, the boy bard of Mallow. And what a leading lady, Shirley Temple O'Shea – O'She's a sight for sore eyes. And what a producer, T Boyle O'Malley, instant impresario and constant pain in the arse. The only time he was in a theatre was when they took his appendix out. Well, I'll stick it no longer. You can come off the boil, O'Malley. Just remember the director is the big cheese. I'm the Big Cheese.

Oliver Riley was T Boyle and sat beside me:

I read: *[T Boyle O'Malley enters from Left.]*
T Boyle: Well the Big Cheese is no gouda, Hickey!
Me: *[O'Malley is a heavy-set man of about fifty. He wears sunglasses . . .]*

"Fuck!" a woman's voice shouted from outside the rehearsal room. There was a northern twang to the accent.

I carried on reading nervously: . . .

"Fuckit!" came again to the vicious click of high heels on the stairs.

"Hold it for a minute, Clare." Dad raised his hand.

I stopped.

Everyone looked at the door.

"Fuckit, anyway!"

76

Then Fidelma Foley came in, huffing and panting loudly. She was wearing stilt-like stilettos and a T-shirt over too-tight leggings. She was oldish, yet had the remains of sexy beauty. "Yous didn't wait for me!"

Dad was patient. "Sorry, Fidelma."

She stood in the middle of the room, hands on her broad hips. "I can't believe this shit!"

Everyone looked at Dad.

He was cool. "We had to go on, Fidelma. We're only booked in here till lunchtime."

"I've been all over town, looking for –" She looked round angrily. "This . . . this kip."

Everyone was shocked into silence.

Only Fidelma would say it. She had wild black hair and black-rimmed eyes, black painted eyebrows, and a pouty mouth. Her outfit did nothing for her, then she was playing a has-been part, so it didn't really matter. I'd say she was Heather's age, or thereabouts. Only much more glamorous. Heather was pretty but ordinary. And losing her figure daily with the bump.

"Yous wouldn't wait!" Fidelma went on childishly.

Dad placated her. "You don't come on till the second act, Fidelma."

She couldn't argue with that.

"I'll go, if I'm not needed," she shouted again.

Dad was firm. "You're *needed* to read the play."

"I can't work *here*!"

Dad's face twitched.

She looked around scornfully. "This is a kip! I'm used to a stage!"

Dad has a short fuse, which sometimes still blows. Like the time he got hysterical about the dog dirt. Any minute now it'd go off again. The twitch was a sign. It was a case of snap, crackle and explosion. Was putting on a play to be fraught with difficulties? Actors didn't seem at all easy to get along with.

Then Oliver Riley, the peacemaker, started singing again, "I dreamt that I dwelt in marble halls . . ."

Everyone giggled.

Even Dad, who held up a hand for silence. "Thanks, Oliver!"

Oliver stopped. He smiled blandly at Fidelma.

Again it diffused the anger.

Then he gently touched Fidelma's arm. "It's only for first week's rehearsal, love."

She looked calmer. "Well . . . "

"We'll be moving to the theatre soon."

"Well . . ." Her eyelashes fluttered. "Will we, Ollie?"

He patted her again. "Yes, lovey, it'll be better there."

He obviously hadn't seen the "Theatre" – the Pigsty wasn't much better than this shabby rehearsal space. But Oliver had a thing for Fidelma from that first day. And she was a man's woman. She calmed down, and sat cosily beside Oliver until it was time to read her part.

After we finished the reading, the whole cast had lunch in a nearby pub. I was feeling bad about my debacle with Bentley. I had messed up completely.

But Oliver winked at me. "You did that well, love, considering what you had to put up with!" He grimaced at Bentley's back.

It eased my hurt feelings. Oliver was to be a ballast of good sense. Throughout the production, he constantly played the role of peacemaker, quieting hysterics with his singing, and nursing bruised egos. From that very first day he drove Ivy home. "A Countess is entitled to a chauffeur," he'd joke.

A pity all actors weren't like him.

Chapter Seven

The cast rehearsed for about ten days in that bleak room on the quays. I'd been in an acting class play once, but didn't know real actors worked so hard. Dad was endlessly painstaking, going over and over scenes, saying, "Take it back," and "From the top."

It was hard work.

Really tiring for the old people.

I wasn't always present as there were things to do for the production – helping the owners paint the Pigsty, getting props, posting out flyers and putting them round hotel lobbies, shop windows, supermarket noticeboards and even libraries.

A NEW PLAY –
Tennessee Tierney has not Lived in Vain
by
Luke Merrill
Opening at the Pigsty, Talbot Street – August 12.

I carried Blu-Tack everywhere.

Most shops agreed to put our flyer in their window. Some put up our poster. A few were difficult, particularly an all-night shop in Rathmines. They refused both. I left, calling them philistines.

An ASM's a jack-of-all-trades.

Still, I was enjoying myself.

And gaining great experience.

I had a cheque book and was in charge of finances. I got weekly DART tickets for our family. And we always had lunch out in a pub. Dad had his pint of diet Coke, while the others drank beer or water. Despite Bentley, there was a wonderful feeling of friendship growing among the actors. Of all working together. I usually joined Dad, Luke, and Katie and some of the others for lunch. Sometimes we went to Mooneys of Abbey Street, or sometimes to the Harp Bar where Dad liked the meat salads, especially the roast beef – ugh.

Ivy went and sometimes Angus.

She brought her own lunch in a small wicker shopping basket, and spreading out a napkin neatly, ordered a glass of water and sat there, delicately eating tiny white crustless sandwiches, not minding who saw her. The pub authorities didn't seem to care.

From the beginning, she focused on Angus. I often sat between them, so noticed that he didn't bother to speak to her. I suppose love can go unrequited at any age. She hardly noticed her chauffeur, Oliver, who was so kind to her, but instead offered Angus a sandwich – which he always bluntly refused.

One day she offered me one. "Ham, dear?"

"Thanks, Ivy." I hated dead pig, but it was impolite to refuse an old woman. Besides the ham was probably processed plastic.

Delicately she placed a pile of tiny triangular sandwiches on a napkin between us. "I'll leave them here, so you can help yourself."

I bit into the sandwich. Immediately my breath went and tears nearly blinded me.

Ivy looked concerned. "What is it, dear?"

"Eh – mustard."

There was nothing else between the slices. As soon as my breath came back and my eyes stopped stinging, I joked the old actress, "Where's the ham?"

Ivy chewed solemnly. "Very bad for one, dear."

"Nonsense!" Angus muttered.

"Ham's probably the safest meat these days," I placated.

Ivy was probably vegetarian too, I told myself, but mustard sandwiches? Grandfather had once made Katie eat them as a punishment. I forget what she did wrong – she usually got away with everything.

Then Angus looked at me – as if to say, *She's a spacer!* I noticed he niggled her at every opportunity.

Luckily Ivy didn't seem to notice. "You have to *imagine* they're ham, dear."

Angus poked me. "Ever hear of a Protestant fire?"

I shook my head, although my dad was Protestant. "What is it?"

"A fire with no coal!" He jeered, shivering artificially. "They sit in their coats."

He was mean to make fun of her. It wasn't the thing nowadays to refer to someone's religion. And his hair looked ridiculous. Today it seemed to be stiffened with hair spray.

"That's a Protestant sandwich," he went on, peering at it.

What was wrong with bread, butter and mustard?

Ivy smiled. She either didn't notice his niggling or didn't mind and always took it good-humouredly.

One day she clutched my arm. "Will you come to lunch on Saturday, Clare, darling?"

"Bring your own!" Angus nudged me, winking.

I ignored him.

"It'll be a *girls'* lunch," the old lady whispered.

I was delighted and accepted, promising to phone her at the weekend, in case something came up. There was Grandfather's garden. And you'd never know if Dad needed something done. He made all sorts of calls on me – buying coffee and packets of biscuits for rehearsals, sweeping the floor, sitting by the door to prevent people coming in. "You're in the book?"

"I've no phone. And I live out in the country."

As she wouldn't be coming in on Thursday, I agreed to send a note if it wasn't OK with Grandfather. "What's the address? Eh . . . it's – Countess Biscovicz?"

She straightened her back. "I'm not Countess Biscovicz!"

"Oh . . ." I was puzzled. Then why did Dad tell me she was? And everyone call her that?

"I'm Ivy, Countess Biscovicz."

"Oh . . ."

"I *am* the widow of a Count. That makes me Ivy, Countess Biscovitz. The present Count's wife is Countess Biscovicz."

"Oh . . ." I remembered Lady Gregory. "Like Augusta, Lady Gregory?" I had read her play, *Spreading the News*, in a book of women playwrights, and had always wondered why her name was in that funny order.

Ivy nodded sadly. "Except the Gregorys were a much more famous family."

I wrote down Ivy's address – The Lodge, 26, Broaddyke Road, Ballinteer.

I hoped she wouldn't forget our lunch.

Here was a famous actress, a veteran of the Gate, the Abbey, and many Shakespearean productions, a woman who had trod the boards with Ireland's greatest, inviting me to lunch. Me, plain Clare Kelly. I felt honoured. I'd never been invited anywhere by an adult. Although Ivy was eccentric, I admired her. To be working at her age was miraculous. She was a sort of role model who'd give me hints. An ideal to aspire to. I wanted to act great roles like her. Be famous and know the famous. Also, I'd never met anyone quite so grand. She was like Countess Markievicz, another Anglo-Irish romantic figure, who'd really lived life. Who'd suffered for her ideals, been imprisoned, loved passionately, and escaped the dreary nine-to-five fate that the majority of people, including Grandfather, admired. Except Ivy was real and not a figure from history. She would tell me stories of her youth. There would be mementoes in her house of her days on-stage, photographs of actors like Michael Mac Liammóir, Hilton Edwards, and maybe Cyril Cusack, whom I'd seen once walking down Leeson Street.

I couldn't get out of grandfather for that Saturday. So Ivy agreed on the following one for our "girls' lunch." Ivy was a complete contrast to Grandfather. Unlike him, she never complained about being old. She was full of hope, and he of pessimism.

But I felt for Grandfather.

I had to keep the weeds at bay. Otherwise they'd take over the world.

That day Dad said casually, "Ask if I can borrow the car, Clare."

I was curious. Was it some ruse to stop Grandfather driving? "What for?"

"For Heather's check-up. She's an appointment in the Rotunda in two weeks."

It sounded too complicated. "She can get the DART."

"No, I want to drive her."

This was unusual. Dad had never borrowed the car before. We weren't car people. Although he kept an international licence for his occasional summer jobs as a tour guide, he didn't drive. He only grumbled about Grandfather driving. Grandfather was the proud owner of a dark blue vintage Morris Minor. Katie and I had christened her Mabel because only a *she* car could look so dumpy and reliable. She had a lovely thin red stripe on her body and all the original fittings, including real leather seats. In thirty years she had only done forty-eight thousand miles. Grandfather polished her weekly and got upset if you looked crooked at her. So he'd hardly agree to anyone else using her.

Especially Dad. But I went to Ranelagh with the begging bowl.

Dad had a way of twisting your arm.

He was certainly taking his new responsibilities to heart. He seemed to care about Heather now. Would it last? What would happen when the baby came? Memories of his drinking were etched on my brain. Like the time he locked Heather out. I'd awake at night to hear them shouting. Then I'd sit at the top of the stairs, listening and dreading the future. Dad would shout bad words. I'd tried to forget all that, but couldn't. The result was I couldn't say the F-word. I could only manage "hell" and "damn."

Grandfather was out shopping that day, so I did the garden as usual.

Afterwards we had tea.

Aunt Brigid kept asking about the play, but he never once mentioned it. I chatted on, telling her she'd definitely be needed once we started. We were clearing up when I asked about the car. "Can Dad have a lend of Mabel?"

He wasn't at all pleased. "You mean a loan?"

I was flustered. I always said the wrong word around him. "Yes, a loan – he wants to borrow Mabel. Heather has a checkup in two weeks."

He frowned. "She's ill?"

"No, she's having a baby."

He almost dropped the tray. "A what?"

"A baby."

"Your father's?"

"The milkman's!" I snapped back.

This completely freaked him.

"Don't be impertinent, Clare!"

Impertinent? I kept quiet, although boiling inside. Was it Dad's? What a thing to say? Who else's could it be? Grandfather'd never given Heather a chance. Not once in all her life. She made one mistake by falling in love with Dad, a Protestant and worse, an American. Now she was accused of sleeping around. At forty plus. What did he think she was?

Aunt Brigid giggled nervously. The worried red spots had appeared on her cheeks. "It's wonderful news, Clare. Imagine une petite soeur?"

I smiled tiredly. I already had one.

"Have they thought of names?" she enquired. "Aoife's nice. Or Niamh."

"They were thinking of Mary, after our President. Or Bill or Hillary – after the Clintons."

Grandfather snorted and Aunt Brigid looked intrigued.

"But Heather decided on Daniel. Or Danielle – after Dad. We're all excited. Katie's absolutely thrilled."

I'd never admit the truth.

Grandfather pursed his lips. "I thought they had some sense."

He was past it, so expected everyone else to be.

"They probably didn't plan it, Alex," Aunt Brigid said coyly. She liked Dad and usually took his side – except when he was drinking.

Grandfather brooded on. He sat there staring into space.

I did the washing up.

When I went to say goodbye, he said, "Is your mother still working in that shop?"

I nodded. He never said Heather's name. Always "your mother." And he always said "that shop," as if there was something wrong with working in a book shop.

"Yes. It's a responsible position," I said. "She has to know all about the book trade."

He grunted. "Never saw her reading anything decent."

I couldn't argue with that. But she knew the book business inside out. Was she to be given no credit?

I was tired of him running her down. No matter what, I'd always take her side. She had no one else. "Most people don't read anything *decent*! They read popular books for entertainment."

He looked at me without speaking. Then he said gently, "What will she do with the baby?"

Hadn't he heard of crèches?

"She has help," I said. "Me and Katie."

"Hmm." He kept staring at me. What was he thinking?

"Can Dad have the car then?"

It was getting late. I had to finish up and be on my way.

Grandfather looked weary. "No, your family has cost me enough."

I wanted to shout, YOUR FAMILY TOO. WE are a family. Why can't you be kind to Heather just once? Can't

86

you see she's a pathetic middle-aged woman with a pathetic lack of confidence? She ran away with Dad, all because of your endless putdowns. What did you do to her in youth?

As usual, I didn't say anything. I took it out on the remaining dandelions. I filled a big black plastic bag with weeds. Then put beer out in saucers – grandfather didn't drink himself, but kept beer in the shed for the slugs. Damn grandfather. He was too mean to piss.

Dad took the news about Mabel calmly.

"I expected nothing from that Muslim patriarch," he said loftily.

Grandfather was a fanatical Catholic. Yet Dad always called him a Muslim. He called him other terrible names: a right wing loony, a mean piss artist, an old fart. But Grandfather had a point. He'd lodged Katie and me for years, footing the bill for our clothes and uniforms for Mount Prospect – Heather's old school, and actually a horribly snobby dump, which had given Katie deep inferiority complexes. Heather went as a boarder at age nine, and it didn't do her any good either. But Grandfather claimed it was the best school in Dublin. He could've spent the money on a better car for himself. But didn't. Mabel was all he had really. He took great pride in her, reverently rubbing her weekly. A person has to love something.

So Grandfather's refusal was understandable.

Then, weirdly, he wrote Dad an extremely polite note, saying of course he could borrow Mabel to drive Heather. It was totally out of character. But I still worried. What if something happened? A crash? Or it broke down? Dad, of course, was unfazed by this prospect and planned to collect the car the day before the Rotunda appointment in a couple of weeks.

Why couldn't they go by DART?

It seemed an awfully roundabout way of doing things. But Dad was worried about Heather. I suppose he wanted to be the good father. God knows he'd a lot to make up for.

Chapter Eight

We moved into the Pigsty at last.

There was loads to do then, getting the place ready. I helped the owners with sweeping, cleaning and painting. Otherwise, when not sitting in on rehearsals, I found props.

We had to find a proper picnic basket for Ivy, a sombrero hat for Bentley and golf shoes for Angus for which I intended to try Oxfam. And Katie's character, Penny Wise, was a sort of cracked, over-the-top, magpie of a set designer who constantly carried objects on-stage and tried to persuade Hickey, the director, to use them. So we needed all sorts of useless junk: a bird cage, a bull fiddle, a deer's head with huge antlers, and a cast iron crock pot.

I had to find these.

Somehow.

As there was no money, it was a question of beg or borrow. I went round the shops with the hat out for contributions. It was a bit like job-hunting, except better. I had something to give back, and offered free tickets to the play plus a mention in the programme in exchange for the loan of a prop.

On the whole people were great.

Stock donated a picnic basket for Ivy's character. The

Royal Irish Academy of Music promised a bull fiddle. An antique shop offered us a deer head with antlers and anything else we might need.

I immediately took a cast iron crock pot and promised to return for the deer's head.

The problem was getting it to the theatre.

I was a vegetarian – what if I met animal rights enthusiasts?

The shop was in one of those narrow streets behind one corner of the Green. So it meant carrying it through the middle of Dublin, down Grafton Street to O'Connell Street and then right into Talbot Street. I liked animals and the head was grotesque. The brown doe eyes, although glass, were plaintive, the antlers soft, like the bare branches of a Sumach tree. How could anyone look at it, never mind touch it? How could anyone have killed it? I thought of asking Dad, but he was too harried. Anyway it wasn't that heavy, just awkward and upsetting.

A job was a job.

I couldn't let Dad down.

So, steeling myself, I collected the horny head on the appointed day and carried it down Grafton Street. People gave me curious looks, OK, but no one bothered me.

Outside Brown Thomas's, someone shouted, "Hey, Clare! Clare!"

I stopped.

"Clare!"

It was Shay.

I was never gladder to see anyone – with his two earrings, his lovely smile and unshaven face. As always, he wore his baseball cap with his Agassi pony-tail sticking out. And a floppy T-shirt over ragged blue jeans.

He ran over and immediately took the huge head from me, holding it up by the horns. "For fuck's sake, whasdat?"

"A reindeer head." I noticed he had a bruise over his eye.

He roared laughing. "Never heard of fuckin' reindeers in fuckin' Ireland."

"Well, some sort of a deer. What happened your head?" I pointed to his forehead.

"Walked into a fuckin' lampost." He stroked the deer's head. "Bambi, poor Bambi."

"It's a prop for Katie."

"For fuck's sake . . ." He gaped into the gentle glazed eyes. "Poor fuckin' bastard."

We set off down the street. With him there, I felt less self-conscious. "Thanks, Shay. I'm a vegetarian."

"Fuck dat. Dese horns are too fuckin' heavy for a girl."

Although small, Shay was muscular and, like the man in the gospel story who carried Jesus's cross, he carried mine the rest of the way down Grafton Street, over O'Connell Bridge and down Talbot Street to the Pigsty.

I suppose that got us together – "the family that prays together, stays together." "People who carry deer's head together, get together."

Or maybe it was because Katie and Jerry had paired off. They were really into each other. It looked so easy. Would Shay ever like me?

We sat together at lunch and he often walked me to the DART after rehearsal. But it wasn't like Katie and Jerry. I was only Katie's leavings, I knew, but wanted to win Shay's love somehow. I'd never gone all the way with a man – in bed, that is. I was reluctant, I don't know why. Wally was *waiting*. He said he didn't want to put pressure on me – that I'd had enough pressure in my life with the parents being off in London, etc., and living with Grandfather. And I didn't know how to break the impasse between us. Anyway, he'd gone for the whole summer, so my feelings for him were on a low simmer. Now I loved Shay. I even bought rainbow coloured condoms in readiness for the big day. I was nervous about doing it. Would it hurt? And what on earth did you talk about afterwards?

I had to impress Shay somehow.

We talked a lot – about music, literature.

I explained that plays were divided into histories, tragedies and comedies. He seemed impressed and kept saying, "For fuck's sake, Clare, is dat right?" Then he'd fall into a reverie, muttering, "I'm gonna make the fuckin' big time, Clare. I'm gonna make alotta fuckin' bread."

He was like Dad.

And funny too.

But awfully accident prone. Things happened to him. Once there were bruises all over his arms. This was from grappling with a lion in the Zoo, he joked.

We started pairing off together to eat sandwiches for lunch in the Memorial Gardens in Parnell Square, in front of the Oisin Kelly sculpture of the Children of Lír. He climbed up on it one day but the keeper told him to get down. Or else we'd walk around Temple Bar, crowd-watching. I told him all about our years living with grandfather, and he told me all about his family.

He lived in a block of flats in Rialto with his ma and da and nine younger brothers and sisters. His ma, who supported his acting, had been in love with Alan Ladd and called him Shane "which he'd changed to Shay. She was like a woman in an O'Casey play, he said. While his da did nothing but call him a nancy boy because of his ponytail and his earrings and his ambition. Shay was a real artist. I'd never met anyone as dedicated. No one in his family had ever been in a theatre, never mind acted in one.

I hinted that I'd love to meet his ma.

He had to fix a time with her – maybe in a week or so.

Did meeting his family mean our relationship was developing onto a more serious level? The condoms were still unused. Shay'd never even kissed me. Never even once tried, or suggested we should be alone together. Maybe he was shy like me? Or he didn't like to mix work and social life? Or maybe he thought I was the boss's daughter and he couldn't.

I studied myself in the mirror. Was it my glasses? My nose was too big. And I had a mole on my neck. I'd finally got my hair cut, but it didn't make any damn difference.

He kept saying I had a convent accent.

Did that mean I was a middle-class snob? Maybe we seemed rich? Dad was inclined to come on strong, act like some big American director when he was one drink away from ruin. But I couldn't tell Shay this. I couldn't tell him Dad was on the dole too, but went early so as he wouldn't meet anyone in the cast. I couldn't say: There's no need to be scared of me. We're poor too. We've had problems.

Shay kept putting me off about meeting his mother. But Ivy kept her promise and invited me the next Saturday for our girls' lunch.

It was difficult to let Grandfather down, so I arranged with him that Katie'd go in my place – after rehearsals. For most of the day, she had to work with Dad and some of the cast.

At breakfast I told her Grandfather was expecting her.

Of course, she grumbled.

I persisted. "Look, he hasn't seen you for ages."

"I hate gardening."

"Just pick a few raspberries for him. Otherwise, they'll rot on the boughs."

She still pouted. "You shouldn't have said I was going."

"He *needs* company. And you haven't seen the dogs for ages."

"OK." She relented, but remained dead jealous about Ivy. "Why's she invited you?"

I shrugged casually. "Dunno."

People usually liked Katie better than me. They couldn't help being taken with such a tall, beautiful, jokey teenager. Her happiness attracted them, I suppose. I knew she wasn't always happy, but other people didn't.

Katie stirred her cornflakes unenthusiastically. "It ain't fair."

I smiled irritatingly. "Who said life's fair?"

She put her elbows on the table. "But I've been rehearsing *all* week."

"You have to make sacrifices for art!" I went to wash my teeth.

She called after me. "But it's Saturday. I have to rehearse all day. Then garden!"

I'd never heard such rubbish. "If you want me to take your part, just say so."

This called her bluff.

I knew it would.

Katie was enjoying her new role. She loved being the centre of attention. And I have to admit she was turning out well as an actress. Dad was working with her and by degrees she was learning the part – I often heard her lines at night. The cast still had books, but that day he wanted to go over some more things with her. She couldn't get the blocking right.

I looked in before I left. "Remember Grandfather's expecting you."

Katie made a face. No matter what she did, she'd always be the favourite. But I was first with Ivy.

"'Bye, I'm off!" I banged the hall door.

All the way into town on the DART and then on the 48A bus to Ballinteer, I imagined what Ivy's home might be like. It was at the edge of the Dublin mountains. Maybe, being titled, she'd still live in a big house, or at least the gate lodge to one. A house called "The Lodge" had a bit of a ring to it.

But 48, Broaddyke Road wasn't in the country at all.

It was an ordinary semi-d in an ordinary housing-estate with a view of the Dublin mountains — exactly the sort of house Katie wanted to live in. *The Lodge* was on a sign at the side of the house, with an arrow pointing to a garden path. You took it round the house to a secret garden full of wild nasturtiums, geraniums and hollyhock. Then you saw Ivy's house in a cluster of shrubs at the back.

It was a caravan.

And magic.

Little steps led to the open door.

I knocked and waited, but no one seemed to be home.

I knocked again.

Still, no one came.

Is anyone there said the traveller?

I was early, but I didn't like to go in, so looked round at the shrubs and flowers. An artist had planted the garden. Nothing was pruned, unlike Grandfather's manicured lawns. Lilypads floated on a pond surrounded by red hot pokers. White and blue and yellow climbers crept over the door and the caravan roof. There were terracotta pots of mint, parsley, and rosemary by the wooden steps. And at the back of the garden, birds perched on the laburnum and fuchsia and even more trees and shrubs I couldn't identify.

I rang the bell again.

This time Ivy appeared, slightly stooped and holding her back.

"Ah, Clare, darling," she wheezed. "You're early."

"Sorry – the bus was too quick."

"It's never too early for you." She winced, straightened up and whispered, "The dogs didn't get you?"

I was alarmed. "Dogs? No."

"Awful little yappers. My landlady doesn't like people."

"Oh . . ."

"She has a lean and hungry look." She waved her hand actorishly. "She doesn't entertain. Whereas I do. Must have people about me. Particularly nice young people like you."

I went red.

"Come in, darling." Still holding her back, she stepped in.

I followed. "The plants look terrific. What do you do to them?"

"Speak firmly to them. And throw some tomato food on them. They love it."

The caravan had been made into a real home, in miniature. "It's lovely here."

"I moved here when my husband died. It was the country then. Before the city started spilling over."

It reminded me of a doll's house. Or the tree house I built when I was small. It was cramped, but had everything – a small kitchen with a table and cooking area. An antique rug, armchairs and an imitation coal electric fire in the wall of the living area. This was on full, although it was a hot summer's day.

"Is it warm in winter?" I asked.

96

Ivy sighed. "It's . . . all right, darling."

There was no place to sit, but she moved her sleepy marmalade cat, "Shoo!" Then offered me sherry from a beautiful cut glass decanter.

The sherry was pretty strong and took my breath away, as I don't usually drink. I'd given it up at Confirmation. Dad's behaviour would put anyone off – so I'd never really started.

Ivy sipped happily, staring at me. "You're so lovely, my dear."

I was amazed. "Me?"

"Yes, your cheekbones are classic."

I reddened. "Katie's considered the best looking in the family."

"She's pretty in a conventional way," she went on. "But you're far more interesting." She sighed. "Youth is wasted on the young."

Before I could say anything, she asked worriedly. "Now, how am I doing, darling?"

"Eh – what do you mean?"

"How's my acting?"

"Fine – you're the most famous in the cast."

She sighed heavily. "*Was*, darling."

"You still are! The others aren't known."

"Oh, Fidelma has a reputation."

"But Angus is only an amateur. You and Oliver are our stars."

She smiled coyly, clutching me. "Hmm . . . Isn't Angus handsome?"

I cleared my throat. It was weird – she really liked him. I suppose the sex drive never goes. But Angus was married and had she not noticed he'd called her a Protestant fire builder? It wasn't the thing nowadays. "Eh – he's OK. He acts well."

97

"Yes, I'm working on getting him an Equity Card." Then, she frowned, wrinkling her papery skin. "But it's so long since I've worked – I'm worried."

"About what? You could act in your sleep."

She clutched my arm. "I get stage fright, dear."

I was amazed. "You?"

She nodded.

Of course, actors got nervous, I knew that. But Ivy? "Look, you're doing fine."

She didn't seem convinced.

It was crazy, me an absolute nobody assuring someone of her fame. We chatted on for awhile, then she served the lunch – vegetable soup and tiny sardine sandwiches. Everything was beautifully correct and we had real linen napkins with roses embroidered in the corners.

"I'm afraid there's no wine," she said regretfully. "You don't mind, darling?"

"I don't usually drink."

She poured me a glass of water and more sherry for herself. Finally I told her about my acting hopes.

She gave me a long look. "You should be careful what you wish for, darling. You might get it."

It was an odd thing to say. "You mean, don't jump into it?"

"I mean just that, be careful. Shaw said that there are only two tragedies in life – one is not getting what you want, the other is getting it." Then she changed the subject. "I notice Mama's *enceinte*?"

I was puzzled. "Eh, what?"

"She's expecting a child?"

I looked away. "Oh, yes. It was unexpected."

"An afterthought." Ivy was matter-of-fact. "Happens all the time."

I hesitated. "Eh – she's a bit old. Forty-three."

"Mama's not old! My mother was forty-three when she had me! A late child's a great blessing."

I hadn't thought of it like that.

"Well, aren't you glad?"

I shrugged. Ivy reminded me of a poem Heather was always quoting about two men looking out of a prison window – one saw mud and the other stars. It was true. I looked on the bleak side. A teacher in school had once said I was too negative. I had to be more hopeful, more welcoming of my new sibling – Mary, Bill, Hillary, Daniel, or Danielle.

As I downed a sandwich in one bite, Ivy stared in shock. "Clare."

My mouth was full. "What?"

She looked horrified. "You don't cut your bread?"

"Oh?"

"There's a knife beside your plate."

"Sorry." I cut the sandwiches into tiny bits and tried to eat more delicately.

"That's better." There was relief in her voice. "Makes it last longer. Young people nowadays are in such a hurry."

Did she need her food to last? I felt downright barbaric. "I suppose it's not as good mannered nowadays?"

She smiled kindly. "It's not manners, darling."

"Oh."

"Morals maketh man."

I was puzzled. "What about woman?"

"Morals maketh woman too."

"We're not as moral now?"

She put down her spoon. "You're so much more moral, darling."

"Really?" It wasn't the answer I'd expected. But that was

99

Ivy. Compared to Grandfather she was thoroughly modern. If only I could get them together. She might make him cheer up.

"There was so much hypocrisy in my youth," she went on sadly. "Everything was covered up. It was hideous."

"It was Victorian times."

Her blue eyes smiled. "Ah no, I was a flapper, darling."

Suddenly I saw her doing a Charleston around a ballroom. I saw young men clustering around her. Chandeliers and log fires. She must have been really something. She still was.

Like a lit candle in a holy place.

So is the beauty of an aged face.

"Well, I'll cut my bread in future."

We both laughed and then had yoghurt and fruit for dessert.

Afterwards, she got down to serious business. "Now, Clare, I've asked you here for a reason."

Her blue eyes looked at me earnestly. To tell me to cut my bread? But there was conspiracy in her voice.

"Yes, Ivy?"

She clutched my hand. "My memory."

"What about it?"

Her voice lowered. "Terrible."

"Oh . . ." Hell, was she was going to forget her lines?

"I need your help, darling."

"Of course, anything –"

She looked relieved and ran a hand though her wispy white hair. "I feel so much better, talking about it. But I'll need help."

"How?"

"To remember my lines."

So this was the reason for our "girls' lunch." I thought for a minute. "Maybe you could have a tape recorder hidden on your person. Wear headphones under a hat."

She shook her head. "Can't work one."

"But I'll show you."

"No, I need my lines on bits of paper. Left around on the props. I'll soon know from the blocking where you can put them. There'll be a piece of paper on the table in a certain colour and then I'll know what to say."

"You can't memorise at all?"

She shook her head sadly. "My age, dear. The memory . . . it goes."

I thought for a minute. "Bits of paper should be easy enough. We could stick them to the inside of your picnic basket. I'll talk to Dad."

She clutched me again. "Oh, *please* don't do that."

"What?"

"Tell your father."

"But –"

"No!" She was suddenly crumpled and really old. "He might not use me, if he thinks my memory's bad."

At this stage he'd no choice. But I didn't know what to say.

Her blue eyes pleaded. "You don't know what a second chance he's given me."

"Yes, but –"

"A new life, Clare. Promise you won't tell your father."

I promised.

All the way home, I thought about what Ivy had said. "Be careful what you wish for – you might get it." I wished to be a famous actor. Dad wished for money and success. Ivy wished for a second chance but, now that she had it, worried about her memory. There was a down side to everything. Still she didn't want to sit at home in her caravan. We all depended on each other. She needed us as much as we needed her.

A feminist felt solidarity with other women, but deceiving Dad was a real dilemma.

Chapter Nine

The cast still had books. So I didn't have to worry about Ivy's memory – yet.

Dad had enough troubles.

Besides, there mightn't be any need to bother him. Ivy was an old pro, so perhaps when we opened she'd know her lines. Or if she didn't, I could leave the notes around like she asked. Or, prompt her from the wings. Ivy was insecure now because it was so long since she'd had a part. On the opening night, she'd be fine. It was my job to reassure her. "Drying" is an actor's greatest fear, even an experienced one can blank in the middle of a sentence.

The play was coming on. We rehearsed daily in the theatre which was almost as dank as the room on the quays. But the weather was holding up, so it didn't matter. It was a heavenly summer, that summer of Luke's play. Sunny days followed by sunnier days. I kept telling myself it'd end. Days passed and it didn't.

One morning we were doing the old people's entrance in Act One. It involved Shay, Jerry, Bentley, as well as Ivy and Angus.

I sat with Dad in the front row.

Bentley and the two boys stood around, waiting. Jerry had transformed his country looks into a swaggering hick playwright, Tennessee Tierney, with a pair of sinister shades.

He was tall with thick curly hair and badly pock-marked skin. He looked down at me through Liam Gallagher shades. "Clare, what ya tink?"

I felt a midget. "They're great."

His part was a send-up and really satirical, so the shades worked.

As Art, Shay played himself, a no-nonsense Dub in jeans and an anorak. He always wore his baseball cap with the ponytail sticking out and had the same unshaven look. I suppose for effect.

I loved him daily more and more. But he still didn't notice me – as a woman. He seemed to have forgotten about introducing me to his ma. Yet he was always polite and always smiled. It's hard to describe an intangible thing like a smile. It was grace, pouring into my soul.

Katie, at least, had chosen Jerry, so there was some hope.

They were still always glued together. He was repeating his Leaving while working in a pub at night. He looked like a tough pop star and she an angel of God.

Then Dad yelled, "Right! From the top!"

Shay ran across the stage, shouting, "They're almost here, outside, clutchin' the area railings, inching along . . . "

Shay's part was to run on and off the stage, keeping up a running commentary like a radio announcer as the old couple came in for their very first morning's rehearsal. He was a natural comic and had me in stitches. Even Dad laughed at Shay's antics as he acted Art's part in his terrific Dub accent:

. . . They're at the door, they're through the door. No, they aren't! Now, they are. No, she's down! Now, she's up. Now, he's down. They're both up. Sort of up. Ah, here they come, here they come, thundering down the home stretch. They're backstage, they're coming through the wings.

Then Bentley came on as Hickey, the director:

Hickey: Tell 'em to use a couple.

Art: And here! They finally come!

Dad jumped up. "Good. Now Shay, you need to be louder on that last line. You build up to it. Try again."

Art: And here! They finally come! They're
            backstage, they're coming through the wings.

"Good," Dad said. "Now, there's a pause in the action."

Everyone waited for Ivy and Angus to come on-stage. But nothing happened.

They waited more.

Nothing.

Being late was certainly in character.

At last Ivy and Angus tottered on with the decrepit graciousness of Perdita and Pembroke. Although it was only a rehearsal, they had transformed themselves amazingly. Angus wore an ancient tweed suit, a thick tweed tie, a crios and a tam hanging rakishly from one side. Also, he carried a large golfing umbrella. Ivy wore a wide, floppy straw hat, held on with a chiffon scarf. Another, much longer chiffon scarf was wound around her neck and trailed after her. Her dress was purple chiffon and she wore a tangle of necklaces. Her knuckles were encrusted with rings, and she carried a gay parasol. She was in character from the roots of her wispy white hair to the very tips of her toes. I could only gape in admiration at her wonderful stage presence and old-fashioned aristocratic good manners. She'd have no trouble remembering her lines.

Bentley came on then:

Hickey:	Ah, you had no trouble getting here.
Pembroke:	None, dear boy, none.
Perdita:	Yes, none.
Hickey:	Well, I'm glad you finally made it. You both all right? You feeling all right today?
Pembroke:	Yes, I leapt up from the arms of Morpheus.
Tennessee:	I thought her name was Potato.
Pembroke:	. . . like a giant refreshed.
Perdita:	Yes.
Hickey:	Good, good, great. Now, today I want to walk through the whole thing.
Pembroke:	Yes, indeed. Yes, let's forge ahead.

Here Ivy coughed delicately. She looked around for somewhere to sit.

Pembroke:	Ah, yes. Would you fetch a chair, Hickey, for Madam. You or one of your minions.

Bentley got the chair for Ivy and put it down in the middle of the stage. Then Dad jumped up, waving his hands irately.

"Not there, Bentley!"

Bentley glowered and dropped it with a bang.

"Not there either!" Dad shouted again.

Bentley pushed up his round glasses peevishly. "For fuck's sake where, then?"

I flinched at his use of the F-word. Why did it always bring back the bad old times when Dad yelled at Heather? Almost everyone in Dublin said it. It was the lingua franca of the city.

Now Dad pointed calmly upstage. "Could you place it on the right, so she can sit *facing* the audience."

Bentley slammed the chair down again.

"Thanks," Dad snapped, glancing down at the script. "All, right Ivy. It's your cue."

Bentley fumed. "It's mine!"

"OK, yours. Go on!"

I watched Bentley's spoilt weak face. Why did he make everything so difficult? Was it because he was so worked up about the Method. Or did he just genuinely hate Dad? He hesitated now as if to say something else, then went on grimly:

Hickey: There! OK? Now, off we go!

Pembroke: Yes, indeed we do, yes! Today, I shall grapple
             with this part – vehemently, violently subdue
             it! Whuff-whuff-whuff! Aghhh!

Perdita: Darling! – Hickey, another chair.

Bentley got another chair for Angus who sank into it, coughing.

Dad jumped up again, "Now, Angus, your coughing needs to be more convincing. Remember, you're in a little worse shape than Perdita." Then he mouthed to me, "What about a coffee, Clare?"

I went to a Talbot Street takeaway.

Dad must be getting a headache. He always needed coffee then.

Coming back to the theatre, I stopped dead.

Aunt Brigid was outside.

Hell . . . she was all done up with the worried red rouge spots in her cheeks and standing on two walking sticks, looking curiously up the Pigsty stairs from the street. She wore a straw sunhat, a long skirt and espadrilles, more suitable for a Spanish beach than a Dublin summer. What did she want? My heart sank – it's another cliché, but that's just what happened. It filled up with pity and fell to the bottom of my chest. I'd promised she could help, but later. It was early days still.

Maybe I could slink back?

But she saw me. "Clare!"

106

I went over, hiding my dismay. "Aunt Brigid!"

She clutched me. "Bon dieu, I've found you!"

I was alarmed. "What is it?"

"I've come to help, but those stairs!"

"Oh . . . Well, it's lovely to see you. Eh – yes, the stairs are definitely too difficult."

"I can manage with a little help, ma petite."

"Oh . . ." I looked at her doubtfully.

"Please, Clare!"

"OK." Aunt Brigid seemed even older out of her normal milieu. She stopped at the first step. "Maybe you shouldn't go any further. Eh, how's grandfather?"

She made a face. "Oh, him! I had to get out of the house."

Were they having another row?

She clutched me, eyes pleading. "Now, tell me what can I do to help, Clare."

I now regretted the weak moment when I'd said there'd be something for her to do. Dad wouldn't be too happy to see her.

"There's nothing much yet, Aunt Brigid."

She was unconvinced.

"Maybe another day," I coaxed.

"There must be something. Helping with props. The front of the house."

"I told you – that's all later! You can help *later*." I took her arm and steered her firmly back to the hall door.

She wouldn't budge.

Her face collapsed, like some sort of soufflé. In a minute she'd cry. "I've come all the way in. And my arthritis is bad today. Don't make me go home."

"We're rehearsing now. You'll be needed later."

"Please, Clare. I'm so lonely."

"You're not. You have Grandfather."

107

She made a face. "He should be in a lunatic asylum!"

I hid a smile.

"I'm old and lonely." Her old voice broke. "And no one has ever loved me."

I was cut to the heart. "I love you, Aunt Brigid."

"Clare," she clutched me. "No one has ever said that."

"Oh, Aunt Brigid!" I sighed heavily. "OK, I'll ask Dad. You want a coffee now?"

She beamed. "Tea, darling."

"Well, I'll just bring this to Dad. I'll get yours in a minute."

Slowly, agonisingly, we went up the stairs into the theatre where they were doing the old people's entrance yet again.

I sat Aunt Brigid down awkwardly, then put Dad's coffee down beside him.

He nodded a thanks, concentrating on the actors.

He hadn't seen Aunt Brigid.

Not yet.

The two old people were in the middle of their entrance scene when Aunt Brigid clapped loudly. "Bravo! Bravo!"

Heads turned curiously to the back of the room.

"Bravo! Bravo!" she screamed again. "Encore!"

"Ah, it's you, Brigid." Dad looked back. Although surprised to see her, he smiled kindly. He was always kind to her. Grandfather was too grumpy, and he reacted badly to that naturally. It was different with Aunt Brigid. "You've come to watch?"

She was delighted. "I'm here to offer support, Daniel."

"Well, OK. Clare'll get you a coffee." He nodded knowingly at me.

"This is going to be a superb production!" Aunt Brigid wriggled on her seat, staring in awe at the stage. "Clare didn't tell me Countess Biscovitcz was taking part."

Ivy bowed graciously.

She had gone pink with delight at the recognition, and seeing her happiness I had to smile myself. Aunt Brigid was probably the only person in the room old enough to remember her.

Dad muttered, "You'll have to keep quiet, Brigid."

"I want to help, Daniel!"

"For now, keep quiet. There's nothing to do yet."

Her face fell again. "So Clare said. Isn't there anything I can do to help?"

"You can help Clare!" he said firmly.

I made a face at Dad. He was offering me up again.

"For now," he put a finger to his lips, "you must be quiet – no talking or clapping."

Aunt Brigid nodded obediently. "Pardonnez-moi."

She stayed that day and afterwards attended nearly every rehearsal. Of course, she was always my responsibility. There was a feeble old woman in our play and a feebler one in real life. It was a case of life following art. I often wondered which was which.

Luckily Oliver always drove her home, along with Ivy. He befriended the old. He also bought drinks for everyone, especially Fidelma. He always tried to cosy up to her in the pub at lunch. At first she took him for granted, although he paid for her food and Babychams. Then she gradually responded. Yet they were both married to others. It was weird – he looked like a tipply parish priest, and she was definitely over the hill. Yet gradually they seemed to get something going. What was the secret?

One day there was an altercation.

We had gone for a drink after rehearsals – Aunt Brigid too. She always ordered a double gin and tonic – which worried me as Grandfather didn't let her drink. But she seemed OK. Just, as I said, she had a habit of staring in awe at people. She'd get carried away and say something personal about them at the top of her voice. Like they were overweight or something. It was quite embarrassing.

She was particularly fascinated by Fidelma, and said loudly, "Elle est jolie-laide."

I nudged my aunt to shut up. It was no use.

"Comprenez – jolie-laide, Clare?" she shouted at the top of her voice.

"Ssshh!"

Fidelma heard, stiffening. "What's she saying?"

"Elle est jolie-laide," Aunt Brigid babbled again.

Oh, God.

Fidelma was furious. "Is she saying I'm a jolly good lay?"

No one knew what to say.

I blushed. "Eh – no!"

"Of course not, pet!" Oliver patted Fidelma's knee.

I leaned over. "It's a French expression –"

"I'm aware of that!"

"Eh, meaning eh – jolly beautiful!" I nodded frantically.

Fidelma was unconvinced.

She glared at poor Aunt Brigid. "She said I was a good lay – I heard."

"Now, pet, don't fret." Oliver hailed a barman for another Babycham.

Aunt Brigid still looked at her adoringly. "No. It means beautiful and ugly –"

"Aunt Brigid!" I elbowed her again. "Please!"

"What is it, Clare?"

"Time to go home!" I hauled her up and out to the street.

Oliver stayed to sooth Fidelma. Then he got his car and

110

drove the old people home. I don't how we'd have managed without him. He was a benediction. A saint.

I ran for the DART.

The platform at Tara Street was crowded. But who was at the far end, necking? Katie and Jerry. I'd know Katie's hair anywhere. He was clutching her bum and she swaying on ghastly high boots which almost touched her mini-skirt.

I went up to them. "Hi!"

"Oh, hi!" Katie turned, mortified.

"Hello there, Clare," Jerry muttered shyly in his sing-song Cork. He was wearing his clear glasses now and had his lumpy serious look.

"Are you waiting long?" I kept my eyes off the bump in his crotch.

Katie was puzzled. "Eh – no. Are we, Jerry?"

You'd think it was a serious question – something which required reflection.

"No." He looked up the line, frowning. "There should be a train soon, Clare."

"It shouldn't be too long," Katie added helpfully.

As we waited, they chatted politely to me, every now and then sneaking loving looks at each other. They were lost to everything. "When a man and woman are in love, they are all the world to each other." I'd read that somewhere.

Jerry came all the way to Bray with Katie. He did this every evening, then walked her all the way to our house – even though he lived on the north side. He couldn't bear to part from Katie. But his influence was good, as she'd given up her stupid riddles.

They related.

Everyone did.

Why couldn't I?

Chapter Ten

Shay finally took me to meet his ma.

It was a lovely summer's day. After rehearsal, we walked up the Grand Canal bank to Rialto. We talked as we went. I remember, I asked what his da did.

He gave me a funny look, then shrugged. "Fuckin' nuttin'"

"He must do something."

He walked on, then looked at me sideways again. "He's in household goods."

"Oh, he sells them?"

"Naw, robs."

I was shocked. "What?"

He was matter-of-fact. "He robs – fuckin' steals."

"I know what it means, but what does he steal?"

"I told ya – household goods."

"Oh . . ."

"Televisions, videos."

"Golly . . ."

Then I said, sounding like Grandfather, "Can't he get proper work?"

"Naw. Too fuckin' old."

"But how old is he?"

"Forty-fuckin'-sometin'."

"That's not old."

Shay stopped and stared into the oily water. There were ducks and flowers floating. "He was on the buildin' in London, but that dried up. Then he came back an' got in with the General."

"The criminal who was shot?"

Shay gave me a despairing look. "Yeah."

This gang leader was murdered just up the road from Grandfather's house. "It's hard on your ma, not having a steady income," I said.

Shay was silent.

I knew about such things. "With so many kids."

He laughed bitterly. "And a fuckin' bastard fuckin' beltin' her!"

"Oh, Shay."

He looked so bitter, I didn't know what to say.

Again I was tempted to tell him about Dad's drinking days, but it didn't seem right. Dad was the director, after all, and had to have respect from the cast. I'd have to keep it till after the play at least.

There was a big black cormorant in the canal. "Look!" I changed the subject.

"Wha?"

"There! A cormorant!" I'd never seen anything like it so near to the city – right *in* the city.

"A wha'?"

"A cormorant." It had disappeared underwater, but then came up again.

Shay rubbed the back of his ear. "Dat's a fuckin' duck."

"It's a cormorant, idiot!"

He walked on, hitting the ground with a branch he had picked up. "Have ya ever seen *The Wild Duck*, Clare?"

I was staring at the bird. "No, but I've read it."

"It's by yer man, Chekhov. A fuckin' great – ."

"Ibsen!"

"Fuckin' Chekhov."

"Ibsen!"

"Chekhov."

"Ibsen!" I persisted.

Shay looked stubborn.

"What do you bet?"

"A hundred fuckin' quid," he said flatly.

"You haven't got a hundred quid. I won't take your money. I'm right. It begins with . . . with Pettersen saying, – 'Say, will you listen to them, Jensen. That's the old man on his feet now, making a long toast to Mrs Sorby.'"

Shay swiped the tops off weeds. "Ah, seen one fuckin' duck, seen 'em all."

He wasn't a bit impressed. How many people could recite the first lines of *The Wild Duck* by heart?

He hit the grass hard. "Pretty boring first line if yeh ask me. Yer man, Chekhov, wrote sometin' about a bird."

"*The Sea Gull.*"

Shay looked up. "Where? I don't see any fuckin' seagulls."

"Chekhov wrote it, idiot."

"Oh . . ." Shay smiled resignedly. "And how does dat fuckin' begin, Miss Know-it-all?"

"One character asks, 'Why do you always wear black?' And the answer: 'I'm in mourning for my life. I'm unhappy!'"

"Hmm. Well, Clare, you're not some fuckin' bimbo, are ye?"

I felt silly. "Eh – no."

Shay was looking at me as if to say, "You show-off." It was true. I'd been trying to impress him.

114

"Well, it's better than Ibsen's line," I muttered, feeling myself go beetroot.

He didn't reply.

"One is exposition and the other jumps right into dramatic conflict."

He still didn't answer.

"Dad says conflict's the most important thing in drama."

He walked on, now making huge holes in the ground with his stick. "Yer'e a fuckin' snob, Clare."

God, was I?

We passed Portobello, Harold's Cross, and walked all the way to the flats, chatting awkwardly about nothing important. The further west we went, the grimmer the landscape got. Car fumes choked the atmosphere. The canal path was littered with coke cans and used condoms. All sorts of debris polluted the water – floating plastic bags and even bits of old cars. How could anyone live here? There were ducks and a few swans, but even they looked unhappy. We entered the redbrick blocks of flats by going under a railing to a scraggy field on which a few sad children played. The flats were all the same, and desperately bleak. Washing hung in the courtyards and one flat was burned out, its blackened windows boarded up.

"What happened there?" I asked.

He shrugged. "Dey like fires."

We passed some children letting off fireworks.

"Isn't that dangerous?" I asked.

Shay shrugged. "Fuckin' is."

Inside, the building smelt of poverty. Graffiti on the staircase wall read: *Al police is priks. Mary is an eget.* And there were more blackened patches on the concrete floor, signs of fires having been lit. "Isn't that dangerous too?"

"Fuckin' is," was all Shay said.

115

A pale boy approached us. He was staring intently at Shay who greeted him, cheerfully waving the stick. "Hiya, Pete."

"You need antin', Shay?"

Shay stopped. "Naw. But tanks."

The pale boy's hand shook terribly. "I gotta nice little number."

"What?"

"I got Es." The boy opened his cupped hand, and Shay leaned over to look, but shook his head.

The friend then jerked his head toward me. "She need some?"

"Naw, Pete." Shay pushed me on. "But tanks."

As we went on up, I said, "He looked ill."

"He's a pusher – HIV positive. A smack-head." Shay was grim. "His whole fuckin' family is."

I glanced back, as the boy hovered by the entrance. A girl in school was expelled for drugs. The nuns said she was doing them, but she wasn't at all. Her rich friend had just ODd, and she had taken her home – that's all. But she was expelled while her friend wasn't. I was head girl, so stood up for her, but it was no use. The nuns have their own agenda. They were into middle class success. The rich girl's father gave a prize for the best yearly English essay. So his kid got off. It wasn't fair. I suppose there were a few wild people in school, but no one had ever approached me. Katie'd been offered a free E tablet – if she sold one – on the way home from school, but my idea of a pusher was still someone from *Miami Vice*, not that pale young boy. How had he turned out like this? But, growing up in such a place, how could he avoid it? How did Shay? We passed a few more odd-looking characters who also greeted Shay cheerfully. One offered him more drugs.

"It's like runnin' the fuckin' gauntlet gettin' in here." He took my hand. "Never come in here alone, Clare."

He'd forgiven me for showing off.

"See that young one?" He pointed to a girl with a baby in a pram.

I nodded.

"Waitin' for a fix."

Then Shay told me all about his brother who was a junkie, hooked on heroin. He tried to come off it by going to a clinic, but there was a waiting list there. Then he got himself arrested, so he'd be sent to prison. But the judge wouldn't send him. He was still on the streets, stealing to support his habit. A younger brother was inside for joyriding.

Poverty was a hopeless place.

How could anyone escape it? They were bringing in free university education, but how would you get in if you grew up here?

"Do they take drugs because of poverty?" I asked.

Shay looked depressed. "It isn't poverty, Clare. No one's that poor! The poverty's in here!" He thumped his chest.

We walked on up the grimy and neglected stairs. When we reached Shay's flat, the door was open. Shay walked right in, as younger brothers and sisters swarmed everywhere.

One looked up and one called, "Ma! Ma, it's Shay!"

His ma was in the kitchen. She was big with short wiry blonde hair and badly scarred skin. Were they the marks of battering? And she looked old, like a grandmother, rather than a mother. But her wrinkled blue eyes were warm. And humorous.

She greeted me, wiping her hands on a plastic apron. "How are ya, Clare?"

I shook hands. "Hello, Mrs Connors."

"Come on in. Shay's always talkin' about ya."

Was he? I smiled nervously. He looked away.

"Yer da's good givin' Shay a chance," she went on.

"Shay's a gifted actor – Dad says."

"Ah, for fuck's sake!" Shay was red but glad. He thumped me gently.

"He told me, honestly," I said. Even if Dad hadn't actually said it, he thought it – I knew. He didn't talk about the actors to me. But I'd seen him in stitches at Shay.

His ma looked proud. "But there's not much chances is dere? Not if ya come from a place like this."

It was true – there were no chances for some. On the other side of the canal was Ranelagh, where Grandfather lived. But it could be a different planet to this flat. Dublin was the most divided city in the world. One half lived in big empty houses and the other half suffered crowded conditions like this. There was a big bed in the sitting-room. Kids and dogs crawled over it and under it, playing or watching TV. The huge set blared in the corner. I remember the Oprah Winfrey show was on all the time I was there. Booming loudly into every corner of the room, so that you couldn't hear your ears.

We were served tea in two matching rose patterned cups.

"The posh china for Clare," Shay joked.

His mother clipped his ear. "Shut up!" Then to me. "Don't mind him, Clare! Have some cake?"

"I'd love some."

As she cut me a big slice of fruit cake, he laughed good-humouredly. "She's posh. Knows all about plays too."

Was I posh? I didn't feel it. I felt awful.

Why had I taunted him with my superior knowledge? It was crazy collecting first lines. It wasn't any different from collecting milk bottle tops. Or telephone cards. No wonder I'd never found love. I was an eejit.

118

After tea and cake, I chatted to Mrs Connors. I told her she'd be getting complimentary tickets.

She shook her head. "I'll pay for dem, Clare."

"No, they're free to the actors' families."

"No, I wanta help yer da."

I was firm. "Our family won't have to pay either."

A toddler in nappies waddled over, wailing. Shay picked her up and hugged her, immediately soothing her. He was an expert.

The conversation moved on to Heather's baby.

Mrs Connors took the toddler. "Shay tells me your ma's expectin' a new one."

I laughed. "Yeah. Totally unexpected."

"Yez'll have yer hands full, won't they, Natasha?" She cooed at the toddler, who now gurgled happily.

Mrs Connors was everything Shay had said. A tigress who totally loved her children. She was a true Dub, with that tough jokey spirit of the city.

After about an hour, Shay said, "Let's split, Clare. You haveta get back ta Bray. I'll walk ya to the DART."

I nodded.

We said goodbye, Mrs Connors promising again to see me at the first night. As we left, there was roaring in the corridor.

A man was cursing horribly. "Where is the fuckin' cunt?"

The C-word was worse than the F-word.

Shay pulled me back and looked nervously at his ma. "Thought he was gone?"

She had paled into silence. The kids were quiet. Only the TV blared.

Then the door crashed open and a heavy man rolled in, swaying drunkenly from side to side. He had red vicious eyes and a completely bald bulldog's head. He fell against a chair, knocking it to the floor. Then he crashed to the floor himself.

God, it was Mr Connors.

He staggered to his feet, roaring, "Where's me dinner?"

The children cried. Dogs growled and scattered. Everyone was terrified. Oprah Winfrey gave out wisdom from the box.

"Where is it, cunt?" He leered at Mrs Connors, who gave the baby to an older girl.

He was dead drunk.

Then he saw me.

"Who's this?"

No one said anything.

He was in my face, spitting. "Who are ya, for fuck sake?"

I was too frightened to speak.

"Who is she?" he roared.

"Shay's mot," one of the bigger kids muttered.

"Shay's mot!" The drunk man roared laughing. Shay went pale as death.

His da kept laughing. Horribly. Leeringly.

"That's a fuckin' good one!" he shouted at last.

I was shaking.

"Yeh nancy boy!" He pulled Shay's ponytail viciously.

As Shay screamed and kicked, the mother threw herself on her husband, hitting his head with a saucepan. In the struggle, Shay wriggled free, grabbed me and ran. "Split, Clare! Split!"

We tore out the door. Behind us kids cried, the dogs barked, and the drunk cursed and swore as Shay's ma yelled, "Ye drunken bowsey, yeh!"

Halfway down the stairs, I stopped for breath.

Shay stopped too, coming back to me.

"Shouldn't we go back and help her?" I gasped.

He had tears in his eyes. "Naw. He's too fuckin' drunk to do anything."

It was the voice of experience.

"I'm sorry, Clare." Shay was trembling.

I put my arms around him, while he sobbed loudly. He was really crying.

"I fuckin' hate him . . . I fuckin' hate him," he sobbed out the words again and again.

"It's OK, Shay."

"Ye won't fuckin' tell anyone?"

"No." I held his shaking shoulders.

"Promise, Clare."

"I fuckin' promise. I'll never tell a fuckin' soul."

I'd said it.

Fuck was a better word than copulation, – more expressive and to the point. "Copulation off!" would sound funny. Wally, my ex-boyfriend, told me that all our physical characteristics and most of our behaviour is ruled by a molecule called DNA, which is a four letter *code*. Four letters couldn't be all bad. Love had four letters too.

I got a letter from Wally, saying how much he was enjoying America. But letters are thin. And now I was mad about Shay. I kept my promise. I didn't even tell Katie about Shay's horrible father. Now I knew why he had so many bruises all over his body. He stayed at home to protect his mother. Our family had had unhappiness too, but his story was much worse. Things had never been so bad for us. Never. Shay's da was a million, million times worse than ours at his worst. Misery existed all around you, yet you never thought about others. You thought you were the worst case. Why did I complain about everything? Things like staying with Grandfather? Grandfather had been so good to us – if it

121

wasn't for him, Katie and I might've been sent to an orphanage. I'd had so many chances compared to Shay. A good education, a summer in France, any book I wanted to read. The play was the only chance he'd ever had. We just had to succeed.

Chapter Eleven

Ten days to first night and everyone was getting nervous –
Katie especially. I was sorry for my jealousy and did everything
to help her. I heard her lines nightly and she now knew them
by heart. Also I coached her in breathing and relaxation and
tried to pass on acting tips, explaining carefully all I'd learnt
about pitch and inflexion in speech.

She found it hard to take in.

So before going to sleep one night, I gave some examples
from my notes. "OK. For a change in emotion, or character,
you use a different pitch. Take, the emotion, fear. If you saw a
ghost, you'd say, 'Who is it?' in a different way, than you'd say,
'Who is it?' if I was coming in."

She nodded.

"Right?" I repeated. "Say it as if you've seen a ghost!"

I studied her face.

"Who is it?" she said quakingly.

"Good! You've seen a ghost!" I read from my notes. "Now
inflexion's the rise and fall of a voice *within* the pitch. There's
simple rising, simple falling, circumflex rising, circumflex
falling and compound rising and compound falling."

She was puzzled.

"Here's simple rising –"

Then Dad called from the kitchen, "Shut up, girls!"

The next morning he said it was all rubbish. You didn't need to be so technical.

As I said, Katie wasn't doing too badly with Penny Wise – she was electric actually. She acted the goofy, intense young girl terrifically well on the whole. We had been round the junk shops with her dressed in character – without telling Dad. Actors did this – Daniel Day-Lewis had stayed in character for Christy Brown after all. And it'd helped Katie. The only thing she couldn't seem to manage was acting sexy. It was curious. Her big scene came at the end of the first act with Shay and Jerry. When the two old people had finished rehearsing and tottered off for coffee, Penny was left alone with the two boys.

One morning Dad was rehearsing them.

"Now, Katie," he said, jumping up. "Penny's very pretentious. She has all these mad theories about art. But she believes them. She's sincere, OK?"

Katie nodded. She pushed back her fringe and glanced quickly at the script.

Dad sat down again. "Right, from the top."

Katie came on, tottering under the weight of a huge bull fiddle. Jerry just stood around, while Shay was doing ridiculous improvs on the other side of the stage – his improvs were a running gag throughout the play.

Penny:	Art, give me a hand.
Art:	Can't they're attached. Besides, I'm doing my tree improv.
Penny:	Then give me a limb, dammit.
Art:	I have elm blight.

Jerry rushed on to help Katie carry the fiddle. As they both hauled it across the stage, he asked her what it was.

124

Penny: Bull fiddle for the Céilí scene.

Tennessee: But there is no Céilí scene.

Penny: Yeah, I have a theory about that.

Then Katie went into her funny monologue:

Penny: Listen, Tennessee, OK, and all, I got a
            problem. My reading of the script keeps
            getting hung up on the words. I have this
            theory that the words are really only
            camouflaging the guts. Now, this play really
            needs to be more externalised, outer directed,
            objectified into a correlated synthesis. So
            you've got to scrap the soliloquy and concrete
            it into the Céilí scene. Neat idea, hunh?

Katie had a slim willowy figure, yet thought she was fat. If
youth was wasted on the young, could beauty be wasted on the
beautiful? Yet she wasn't just a pretty face. You'd absolutely
never know this was her first time out. I laughed as she
continued to lecture Tennessee:

Look, did you ever see my mime version of *Hamlet*? It
revealed things nobody ever suspected were in the play
before. And I can do that with any play. Even yours.
Just grope beneath the flabby verbiage and what do you
find? Basically, you find four fundamental existential
attitudes. Look, I'll illustrate.

She grabbed Shay and dragged him downstage. Then arranged
his arms and hands prayerfully upward, and pushed his mouth
into a smile.

Penny: See! Attitude One – Ecstasy.

Tennessee: He still looks like a tree.

Katie arranged Shay into other attitudes of rage, horror and
finally, lust, at which Shay's character pulls away.

Penny: Attitude Four – Lust!

Art: Hands off!

Penny: Well, I'll show you lust later.

This was where Katie always stumbled.

Dad jumped up. "Katie, hold it! Your character's puzzled, but basically too innocent to know that Art's gay. OK? Now, be more vampish."

She nodded.

It *seemed* like she understood.

"Right, that line again," Dad went on.

Katie said the line in the same flat voice, "'Well, I'll show you lust later'".

Dad stood up again. "Now, Katie. Put a bit of sex into that. Remember, you fancy yourself as a seductress!"

"'Well, I'll show you lust later,'" she repeated flatly.

"Katie!" Dad was getting mad. "For Christ's sake! You're trying to seduce him!"

She tossed back her hair rebelliously. "What?"

"Now, do it! Seductively!" He wiggled his hips, imitating a sexy model, walking the ramp.

She said the line in the same monotonous voice.

Dad was on his feet again. "No, Katie! No!"

What was wrong with her? Why couldn't she do it?

Dad lit a cigarette and inhaled slowly, patiently. "Katie. Just be yourself, OK?"

She rolled her eyes upward. "What do you mean?"

"I mean, imagine it's Saturday night and you're out on the Esplanade!"

She just stood there, her arms folded woodenly. I saw Jerry fuming in the wings. He looked ready to pounce on Dad.

"You're *able* to do that?" Dad said sarcastically.

"What?"

"Be seductive!"

At this she ran off the stage. "You're sexist! You're sexist!"

Dad went white with anger. "Clare, tell her to get her ass back here!" He hissed out the sibilant.

"Oh, Daniel!" Aunt Brigid thumped her stick from the back row. "Ass? What a vulgar word!"

Dad turned his head. "Be quiet, please!"

"Daniel!" Our aunt staggered to her feet. "Behave!"

"You behave, or you'll have to leave!"

She ignored him, dragging herself up and hobbling after Katie. "Tyrant! Tyrant! Ma pauvre petite."

Dad *was* a bit much, but I was afraid to argue with him. Instead I went after Katie, waving at Aunt Brigid to sit down. "I'll look after her."

She stopped and flopped down, exhausted. "Oh, well, all right."

Jerry was beside me next, looking anxious. "Can I talk to her?"

I didn't want them both walking out. "No!"

He still hovered. "She needs me."

God, he really loved her.

I pushed him away. "She'll be OK, Jerry."

My sister was crying in the loo behind the stage. It was unisex and there was a cracked wash basin with a cracked mirror. And a strong smell of pee.

I knocked. "What's up, Katie?"

She let me in, wiping her eyes and smudging the eyeshadow everywhere. "He's picking on me."

"He's not. He's directing."

"One minute he says, 'Be pretentions!'"

"Pretentious."

"That's what I meant. And next, he says, be me – be *sexy*?"

I was gentle. "What's wrong with that?"

She stared at me, outraged.

"What is it?"

"I'm *not* sexy!"

I tried to take this in.

"Mes enfants!" Aunt Brigid then called from outside the door. "Can I help?"

Why didn't she go away? "No, Aunt Brigid."

"Are you sure?"

"Yes," I yelled back. "Tell Dad Katie'll be back in a minute."

The old woman muttered something inaudible. But I could hear her stick scraping the floor as she went off.

Katie was crying like a kid.

I tried to console her. "Come on, stop."

She wouldn't. I said nothing more. Did she really believe that she wasn't sexy? Or beautiful? Didn't she ever look in the mirror? She was so damn beautiful it nearly made me cry as well. Oh, not from jealousy, not any more, it's hard to explain, but beauty always makes me cry. Beautiful skies, the full moon, the sea, poetry, and Katie.

"I'm *not* sexy," she sobbed.

"I know. You're to *act* it."

She didn't answer for a minute. "Oh . . . But why doesn't he pick on the others?"

"Because this is *your* scene."

"My scene?"

"Yes, in most plays if a writer is any good, he'll give each actor a scene. That one's yours."

"Oh . . ."

"Come back and do it."

If she'd had any experience, she'd know what directors did. But she didn't. She just stared miserably into the cracked mirror, her big eyes black with smudged eye make-up. "I hate acting."

For half a second, I was tempted. If she didn't go back, maybe I could be Penny. But it would upset Dad too much. So I put an arm around her, coaxing. "Come back, Katie, please."

Why didn't I use life's opportunities? Here was my slice of life, and I was passing it up.

"You OK, Katie?" Jerry called in his deep Cork.

She smiled. "Yeah."

"She's OK," I called.

Then Dad thumped angrily on the door. "Girls! Get back in here!"

God, he was going to blow everything with Katie.

"Get back here this minute!"

He wouldn't talk to any of the others like that. Only to his children.

When we came out, Jerry put an arm around her. His kindness was just what Katie needed. Luke was there too, looking grim.

He flattened his hair worriedly. "You OK, Katie?"

She nodded, embarrassed.

He stared pointedly at Dad. "You're doing a fine job with that character."

Dad humphed sarcastically.

They'd obviously had words and didn't look at each other. But Luke's support had cheered up Katie. She went back and made some effort to obey Dad's instructions. As she vamped up the part, I sat with Aunt Brigid, in sort of stunned shock. All my theories about Katie's sex life might be wrong. I didn't know my own sister. No wonder — there was no communication in our family. No one ever talked about important things. I had seen her necking Jerry in the station.

129

But could it possibly be that she'd never done it either? When all the time I'd been worrying about her getting AIDS? How did she have all the boyfriends then? Why did Jerry almost faint with love when he looked at her? It was a puzzle.

Katie finally did the scene better.

Oliver, who had come back to drive Aunt Brigid home, clapped loudly and complimented her acting. "Your sister's a good little actress."

I nodded. "She certainly is."

It was as if he also knew she needed praise after Dad's stupid bullying. Yet he hadn't been there. But that was Oliver – kind. That day he was more dressy than usual. His shoes were new suede, and his cavalry twill trousers were pressed neatly. But he was more redfaced than usual. Was he an alcoholic like Dad? Or was it a medical condition? High blood pressure? Some skin condition?

"Katie'll be a leading lady one day." I said proudly.

He looked at the stage. "Maybe."

"I'm hoping to be a character actor."

His blue eyes bored into me. "You want to act, Clare?"

"Oh, yes. I've applied to the Samuel Beckett Centre in Trinity."

"Have you now?"

I didn't say I hadn't been called back for a second interview. It looked bad now.

Oliver went on studying me. "Character actors go on longer. I still get parts. I wouldn't, if I'd been a leading man."

Maybe there were compensations for being plain.

Then he looked anxiously behind him. "Have you seen Fidelma?"

He usually made a date to drive her home.

"I think she went home," I said.

He looked disappointed. "Ah . . . I'd better take your aunt then." And he went over to Aunt Brigid.

Fidelma had stood him up again. What did he see in her? She must have something nice about her, although I had yet to detect it.

Dad remained grumpy, so, feeling sorry for Katie, I took her for a fry-up in Bewleys after rehearsals – Jerry was working in the pub that evening. Then we were going to the pictures for her birthday treat – a rerun of *Four Weddings and a Funeral*, as she liked Hugh Grant. He's a wimp and it didn't surprise me at all that he had to pay for a woman. I far preferred Kenneth Branagh, or the Americans – Tom Hanks and Tom Cruise. But it was Katie's night out.

We'd got our food and were seated under the stained glass window in Bewleys of Westmoreland Street's big airy no-smoking room. All round us were artificial trees, the clatter of cups, clink of cutlery and chatter of Dubliners. Katie was tired and tear-stained. I hated to see her like that – crushed. I even missed her stupid jokes. But she seemed to have given up that habit.

"I love you, Katie," I said suddenly.

She held her fork in mid-air. She stared in amazement. "Are you sick?"

"No." I chased a mushroom round my plate.

"You must be!" Her mouth was full.

"It's just . . . we don't talk enough."

She shrugged and went on eating.

I didn't say anything for a minute. "No one ever told Aunt Brigid they loved her."

Katie frowned in bafflement. "Was she never engaged or anything?"

"I don't think so. But she didn't mean that. She meant Grandfather, her parents. No one in her whole life."

"Golly," was all my sister said and went on eating.

We'd finished the huge greasy fry when she suddenly said, "What did Dad mean, 'Imagine it's Saturday night and you're out on the front'?"

"He meant, you know . . ."

"I don't!"

"I suppose, he meant – act like you're with Jerry."

She was puzzled. "But why Saturday night?"

God, she was thick. "That's the night you're mostly there – during school. Of course, you're not out nearly every night now."

"But what am I supposed to be doing?"

I shrugged. "Dunno. Whatever you do?"

She threw her fork on the plate. "I don't *do* anything!"

"You must do something."

"What?"

"*It* . . ." I whispered.

She looked innocent, just like Dad. "*It?*"

I was getting impatient. "Oh, Katie, stop acting dumb!"

"I don't know what you're talking about!"

"You haven't done it yet?"

"Done what ?"

"IT!"

"It?"

"Sex then? Have you had sex?"

She flicked back her hair primly. "Of course not!"

I stared in disbelief.

"You mean . . ." She peered right in my face. "You think I sleep with people?"

"No!" I looked away.

She was furious. "Jerry loves me! He respects me!"

So much for my theories. You just never know anyone. And I had Katie married to Jerry, myself to Shay. Ivy to Angus, and Fidelma to Oliver. That was four weddings. I just hoped it wouldn't be a funeral too.

Chapter Twelve

On the day of Heather's test, Luke took rehearsals. Normally he left everything to Dad, but he had notes for the cast and wanted to go over a few things.

Dad had collected Mabel from Ranelagh the previous evening. Then first thing in the morning he drove Heather to the Rotunda Hospital in Dublin. I couldn't help being impressed by his new attitude of responsibility. He was really looking after Heather. It looked good for the future.

The test was fine. Everything was OK.

It was a girl.

Our new sister, Danielle, was due in five months, according to the hospital, and all was well. Heather didn't have to worry about a thing.

It was a great relief.

Then something awful happened.

After all the fuss about borrowing her, Mabel was nicked.

I knew it. Don't ask me why, but I felt in my bones that things would go wrong. And they did: when Heather and Dad came out of the Rotunda, she was gone.

Neither a borrower nor a lender be.

Although Mabel had definitely been there while Heather

was being examined, because Dad had gone out for a smoke and had seen her – he was back on cigarettes, openly now, thanks to Luke, who never stopped.

So the parents came home by DART and shanks mare, pretty depressed. Firstly, there was losing Mabel, then the problem of finding a policeman in Dublin to even report the theft to. Heather got an instant asthmatic attack, so Dad left her in a chemist in O'Connell Street, buying Ventolin, and finally found that garda station beside Busarus. The guard on duty shrugged. It happened twenty times a day in Dublin, he told Dad. Joyriders took cars for speeding. It might turn up or not – he couldn't say. They usually did, after being involved in a couple of jobs. The city's crime rate was terrible – all due to drugs. Vandals had to feed their habit. It was unsafe to walk down O'Connell Street in broad daylight, never mind leave a car in Parnell Square. Didn't he know that? He should've used a supervised carpark. There was one in the area. Where had he been all his life?

I'd often wondered the same.

"I gotta sinking feeling, Clare." Dad blinked innocently. "I shouldn't have been surprised. But I was."

Still it was bad luck and the parents were scared to face Grandfather. Dad just couldn't. And I didn't blame him.

So I was sent.

"I'm sorry, Clare," Heather wheezed, as I left.

She had two cucumber slices over her eyes to ease a migraine. She'd made the discovery by accident when using the vegetable as a remedy for wrinkles. Dad planned to patent the idea. He said when Irish people bought water, they'd buy anything.

"It's OK," I muttered miserably. It wasn't Heather's fault.

She removed one slice. "There was nothing about this in

134

my horoscope. '*At last you have assembled the pieces of the puzzle and are able to see the full picture. . .*' was all it said. What could that mean?"

I shrugged. "Dunno."

Heather looked miserable. She put back the cucumber slice. "I'm sorry to put this on you."

I was sorry too, but didn't say. Especially as I hadn't done anything in Grandfather's garden for weeks. He was going to be mad about that too.

Heather grabbed her novel and headed for bed.

As I left, Dad just raised his eyebrows hopelessly. "Thanks, pumpkin."

Why was our family so unlucky? Was it something to do with our collective birth signs? I was Aquarian like Heather, the sign of innovation. Dad, a Sagittarian, was someone who misread situations. While Katie was a Capricorn and rarely objected to change.

Grandfather was Gemini and wise. But a terrible misanthropic pessimist. He'd probably rant and rave now and who'd blame him? First the baby and now this nasty surprise. He was over eighty and had to go to a friendly doctor in Ranelagh to get certified fit for car insurance. Dad was right – he probably shouldn't be driving, now he'd got his wish. But Grandfather only used Mabel once a week for the shopping. He drove up to the Quinnsworth in Rathmines. He'd have to get things delivered now. He didn't walk well either, and wouldn't be able to go anywhere. I felt so badly about Mabel, I had to tell him quickly. If only it was yesterday and all this hadn't happened.

But you can't go back.

The dogs yapped when I rang Grandfather's bell.

Aunt Brigid opened the hall door, immediately grabbing

135

me and pulling me up the stairs. "Clare, ma petite, I want you to decide what I'm to wear to your father's play. I've bought two new dresses in the summer sales."

The dogs jumped on me.

I batted them off.

God, she was always buying things. What did it matter how you looked at her age? "I have to talk to Grandad, Aunt Brigid."

"Brigid, s'il vous plaît." She pulled me up again.

I stood my ground. "Oui, *Aunt* Brigid."

"Oh, Clare. You make me feel old."

I felt impatient. "You are old, Aunt Brigid!"

She was just like Heather, never facing up to things.

"Don't say that, Clare. I'm in love."

"Who with?"

"That darling man – Oliver."

I held back a smile. Did the human heart never change? Did people never stop hoping for love?

She babbled on about her dress. "Voilà! I have a pink cotton or a blue silk? Now which?"

I was sorry for calling her old. "Maybe the cotton."

"Pense-tu?"

"Oui, Brigid. The good weather's meant to last and silk might be too hot."

"D'accord! C'est tres chic. Vous êtes très gentille, Clare. Now, what're you wearing? BT's have a wonderful sale."

My aunt was always trying to get me out of jeans and docks and into a pretty dress. She constantly bought me the most useless presents – pretty embroidered blouses and pleated skirts. I wasn't the type. Katie wasn't either, but she had no scruples about hacking the end off anything Aunt Brigid bought her. Or else changing it.

"I don't know," I said.

I didn't care either.

"You'll have to wear a dress." She gestured with her hands. "I saw something for you."

I hated dresses. "OK. But I've got to talk to Grandad now."

Finally she let me go.

He was in the old lean-to conservatory, looking lovingly at his plants – geraniums, and impatiens clashing and competing with each other, a riot of well-tended reds and purples and pinks, in old clay terracotta pots on the old terracotta tiles.

He looked doddery. I'll always see him in his big straw hat, old grey cardigan, and navy blue canvas shoes, standing with the watering can. And always remember my dread.

"Ah, Clare." He seemed glad to see me – which made things worse. He probably thought I'd come to do the garden.

"Grandad," I blurted. "Something's happened."

He paled. "Katie?"

"No, Grandad."

"Your mother, then?"

"No, Mabel."

It took a second to register. "My car?"

I nodded.

He sighed in resignation, sitting stiffly into the squeaky wicker chair with its faded blue cushions. "Crashed?"

I sat down too. "No. Stolen – from outside the Rotunda."

He didn't speak for awhile. "She belonged to your grandmother. She's thirty years old this year."

I was puzzled. "That's just it. The guards said she was stolen for a job. But who'd want her?"

"Clare! She's a collecter's item."

You could say that again. "But she rattles at over twenty-five miles an hour. Anyway, Dad's sorry. He reported it. They said it might turn up in a few days."

Grandfather looked sad and old. I waited for him to say that the human race should be scrapped and a new mould made. Or that thieves should be eradicated, along with all the weeds in the world. Or that they should bring back the cat. That vandals should be flogged – one thing Grandfather never said was who was going to administer the cat. Him maybe? Or the unemployed? I'd heard that suggested on the radio once.

Finally he sighed wearily. "Why didn't your father come himself?"

"He was afraid," I blurted.

"What?" He looked surprised. "But it's not your father's fault."

I was puzzled by his attitude. "Eh, no."

"It's the times we live in."

Grandfather wasn't taking it too badly. But was it really worse times now? What about people dying of diseases long ago? Surely life was getting better because people were living longer? But according to Grandfather it's quality not quantity. He often said he'd commit suicide, only he was afraid to meet his Maker. I'd say it might be the other way around – his Maker might be afraid of him. Heather and Dad certainly were.

He said nothing more for awhile – just sat there worrying.

I sat there too, staring at the cacti. He had a whole shelf of them – horrible prickly things that attacked you if passed too near. Why had Dad borrowed Mabel? Why hadn't he used a car park?

Then Grandfather broke the silence. "I'll ring the insurance company. They'll let me hire a car. Yes, that's the solution. It was good of your father to drive Heather. How is she?"

"OK . . . She's OK."

"And the baby?"

"Fine . . ." I almost fell out of my chair.

His old eyes softened. As I said, he got gooey about *other people's* babies. Now he was being so nice, completely different. Was it senility? You could never predict *anything* in life. Here was Grandfather, actually praising Dad, asking for Heather, calling her by her name, not THAT WOMAN, or YOUR MOTHER.

"It's a girl – due in five months. Heather mixed up the months. She didn't know she was pregnant for the first month. Thought she was putting on weight. It was a shock at her age."

He looked right at me. "Am I that fierce, Clare?"

I was shocked now. "Eh – what?"

"Is Heather afraid of me too?"

"What?"

"I asked a question, Clare."

"Yes – what?"

"Stop saying what!"

He went on before I could answer. "She was such a pretty child."

I couldn't say anything.

His old eyes were watery. He rubbed them now. "It's a terrible thing to send a small child to boarding school."

Heather had gone to Mount Prospect at nine.

"But your grandmother tired easily."

Heather said she'd hit the bottle, and that was why Grandfather couldn't abide drink. Wouldn't have a bottle in the house.

He was still staring back over the years. "She was only a mite."

"But Heather enjoyed it," I said. "She's always telling us

139

about an old nun who read to her – *The Secret Garden* and that."

He shook his head. "We were strangers ever afterwards. Then she met your father . . ."

That was years later. "But Heather's fond of you."

"No, she doesn't forgive me."

Here was my chance to communicate but I couldn't. I couldn't tell him how mean it was never to say her name. Always to call her "your mother." It was probably true that Heather didn't forgive him. She had gone to boarding school for years. Was that why there was no communication between father and daughter? Our family's problems had probably started back then. Then Heather had fallen in love with an American boy, and instead of liking him, Grandfather had got disgusted with her life. He wanted her to get a separation, *a mensa et a thoro*, something like that. But Heather loved Dad. For years she'd taken so many pills – uppers, downers, in-betweeners. It was your fate if you lived through the sixties. They both used to get high: Dad on drink; Heather on sleeping pills. For all of my childhood she was lost in a maze of Mandrax. It was worse than smoking dope and probably affected Katie and me. There might be something wrong with our brains – something like foetal alcohol syndrome. Because we didn't really communicate either. That was obvious.

"I was ungracious about Heather's news." Grandfather smiled sadly. "I'm sorry."

I couldn't believe it. Was he going senile?

We both stared at the geraniums in embarrassment. Why wasn't he giving out to me about the garden? The dandelions were back. I could see them from where I sat.

Then he said, "I was also ungracious to you, Clare."

I sat up straight. "How?"

"Oh, saying you girls cost me. Forgive me, my dear."

I shrugged. "But it's true. We did – think of all those bags of crisps Katie gobbled."

"You girls were my greatest blessing." His old voice broke. "The best thing in my life."

I didn't know where to look.

"The years like great black oxen tread the world," he quoted solemnly. *"And God the herdsman goads them on behind, And I am broken by their passing feet."*

"But Grandad," I mumbled.

What was it? Was he dying or something horrible? He was always saying he and Aunt Brigid would have to go into a nursing home one of these days. It was only a matter of time. He'd already booked one in Glenageary, but I wanted him to change to Bray. It was full of nursing homes and the old people looked quite happy tottering up and down the road on walkers. Grandfather had a dread of being incapacitated, of not being able to do things for himself. His biggest fear was of flies landing on his face after he was dead, so I'd promised to bat them off – although I'd never even seen a dead body and dreaded seeing his. But he was OK now. So was Aunt Brigid. But she worried about dropping dead too, in soiled underwear. Or about her hair roots showing up white in her coffin. I promised to dye them blonde. No matter what, you always have worries. Even after you're dead.

"Now, I can't invest in any foolishness," he went on slowly. "But – if Heather needs money for the baby . . . I'll cash some Post Office certificates."

He was going senile.

Definitely.

We'd never wanted for any necessity, but he was never *flaithiúlach* in any sense. Not ever. He hated waste and recycled and reused everything. He even darned our socks to save money. He had once knitted himself a cardigan out of dog hair. Now he was offering to commit the mortal sin of spending capital. After we'd lost his beloved Mabel.

I felt awful. "No. It's OK, Grandad."

He frowned. "You're sure?"

"Yes, the hospital's free."

Heather would say the same.

She was in bed when I got home. Her bedroom door was shut and all the lights were out. The house was in utter darkness. Dad must be out with Luke, because there was no sign of either. Or Katie, but she was probably out rocking the night away.

I read in bed. It was a while since I'd had the chance. Lately I fell asleep immediately, and during the day there was usually too much noise in the house.

I was asleep when someone started shrieking.

Heather.

God. Was Dad hitting her?

But he didn't seem to be in.

I jumped up and ran into her bedroom.

The reading light was on and she was hidden under the duvet, sobbing. I called from the doorway. "What is it?"

She kept sobbing.

"What is it?" I went over and touched her shoulder..

She could hardly speak. "A – moth, Clare!"

I jumped into action. "Where? It's OK! I'll kill it."

Heather was mortally afraid of moths. It was a weird phobia. They were all over the Bray night, but she'd left the light on and the window open, so what did she expect?

It was dive-bombing her reading lamp. At first it wouldn't land on a hard surface. But I squashed it after a few tries.

142

She was still under the covers.

I touched her shoulder again. "It's OK."

She peeped out. Her face was white, her hair dishevelled. "You're sure?"

"Yeah!" I laughed. "You can come out. I'll close the window."

She sat up shakily. "Thanks, Clare."

"I'll make you a cup of tea."

"I must've fallen asleep. I awoke with that thing on my face." She shuddered in terror. She was as bad as Grandfather.

I was puzzled. "But they're harmless."

"I know." She was breathing quickly and lightly. "You're so calm and capable, Clare."

"It's only a little moth."

She looked at me nervously. "Eh – how did Grandad take the news?"

I shrugged. "OK. He said it was the times. Criminals should be flogged. The usual . . ." I paused. "He asked about the baby."

Heather made a face. "I was afraid to tell him."

"He was OK. He's mellowed." I sat on her bed. "Maybe you should tell him things."

She said nothing for a second. Then sighed heavily. "It's too late for that now. You can't just start communicating at this stage."

"He thinks you don't forgive him for your childhood."

"Did he say that?" Heather looked amazed.

"Did you hate boarding school?"

She laughed. "No! When he first came to see me, I remember thinking how much I missed him. He looked so strange in the strange surroundings – the parlour. That's what we called the room where we met our parents. But when I was older, I was glad to get away from him. And that miserable house."

143

She didn't say anything more. Or anything about her mother. I made her a cup of tea, thinking how much I liked the Ranelagh house. But the twain would never meet. Life was one big misunderstanding. Heather pretended to be cheerful, but deep down she had terrible fears. Moths reminded her of something scary in her childhood. I knew all about psychology from reading Aunt Brigid's copies of *Reader's Digest*.

Mabel didn't turn up.

And as she was "missing," the insurance company wouldn't hire another car for Grandfather. It was something to do with the small print on his policy which he hadn't read – I forget exactly. It was curious. Who'd taken Mabel? Everyone said fast cars were usually nicked. '95 registered BMWs, not museum pieces like Morris Minors. Was the tubby little banger now involved in a life of crime? It had seemed so terrible when it happened, but Dad shelved it – along with everything else – even Heather's baby, as the play had completely taken over our lives.

Chapter Thirteen

"How much is a Wonderbra, Clare?" Dad screamed the next morning in the DART.

I nearly died. "What?"

"A Wonderbra?"

"Eh – what?"

"A Wonderbra. How much would it cost?"

I shrugged. "I dunno."

Couldn't he keep it down? We were on the way into rehearsal. The train was packed with morning commuters and rowdy Spanish students with packed lunches. They babbled at each other across the aisles, but the middle-aged woman opposite smiled faintly – she'd definitely heard him.

I stared past her out the window to the sea.

Dad's forehead wrinkled right up to the bald bit. "Roughly?"

"Eh – roughly what?"

"Clare!" Dad was exasperated. "*Roughly* how much is a Wonderbra?"

"I'm not sure."

The woman now caught my eye. Other people looked too. Some were laughing. But Dad was oblivious to it all. Was he going funny? From losing Mabel, the strain of production, dealing with difficult actors? Some of ours were awfully demanding. Bentley especially was a spacer, and Fidelma always had some stupid petty demand – she wanted her wig dressed, special panstick make-up.

I looked deliberately at my half of *The Irish Times*.

But there was no shutting him up. "Will you buy me one, Clare?"

I felt my face drain.

Dad cupped his hands over his chest, making a bust. "About like this."

I nodded warily.

I tried to think of something else. Dalkey Island came into view. Already kids were playing on Killiney strand. Heather'd brought us there years ago, but I'd never owned a bucket and spade. It'd look funny if I got one now. All summer, I'd remembered the French boy we saw that night. He was too old for sandcastles too, yet he didn't care. There was a pink light on the water. But instead of enjoying the waves, I felt seasick. Perhaps global warming had already begun as the summer had held up endlessly. A little light rain had been forecast, but it was day after day of sunshine. How long would it last? And what if Bray flooded eventually? The seas were meant to rise from CFC gasses. They'd push the Gulf Stream off course and make us colder than Labrador. Grandfather cared, but said he'd be dead, and anyway Ranelagh was above sea level. Dad always said he'd build his blasted raft. While Heather, typically, said it was all that hairspray in the sixties. Which made Katie immediately squirt more. She, of course, didn't care either. She just loved the sun.

"Clare!" Dad interrupted my thoughts.

I dived back into my newspaper, pretending not to hear.

We were opening next week. Definitely the strain was beginning to tell. He was smoking over two packets a day now. But this bra stuff was more serious.

He dug into his wallet pocket and gave me the cheque book. "Clare, here!"

I grabbed it.

"Will twenty cover a Wonderbra?"

"Yes!" Why didn't he shut up?

The woman opposite caught my eye again. She looked intrigued.

Should I tell Heather? It might be too much of a shock with the baby coming. Thank God, Katie was talking to Luke at the far end of the carriage and was well out of earshot.

"Are they padded, Clare?" Dad yelled as we approached Dalkey station.

"I don't know." I hardly ever wore a bra. It wasn't for feminism or anything, I just didn't have anything to put in one. A crop-top did me.

"Eh, what size do you want?" I whispered nervously.

He sculpted lascivious breasts. "Maybe this big."

"OK." God.

"With – you know – an uplift?" He held up his imaginary breasts.

The train had stopped. Everyone was looking now.

"Make sure it's low cut, Clare."

I nodded.

When we were moving again, I whispered, "Heather might have one."

He shook his head vehemently. "No. Too small."

I stared sightlessly ahead. If Dad was a secret cross-dresser, Heather should definitely know. But should I tell her? She had morning sickness now and was beginning to look worn. It couldn't be easy carrying on her job, and this news might cause a miscarriage.

I sneaked a look at Dad. He seemed normal. I'd certainly always thought he was. It's not that I was intolerant, or anti-gay or anti-transvestite or anything. It was just that a *dad* is different.

He caught my stare. "Better ask Fidelma."

"What?"

"About the bra size!" He frowned. "Clare, wake up!"

It's true that I'm terrible in the morning. "Eh – why ask her?"

"It's *for* her!"

"The Wonderbra?"

"Yes!" Dad looked ready to shake me.

"Oh . . ." I took a deep breath, a deep breath of relief. Then it hit me. "The bra's for the play? For Fidelma?"

He nodded, speaking slowly, as if to an idiot. "Yes, Clare. Why else would I want it?"

I grinned happily. "I dunno. Maybe for Heather."

He hmmphed.

Then I said, "But doesn't Fidelma have a bra?"

"Apparently not!" Dad sighed irritably. "We have to buy her one." He rustled his paper and went on reading.

We'd had to buy £60 golf shoes for Angus – there were none in Oxfam or any of the secondhand shops. At least a bra for Fidelma was cheaper than shoes. Now I only had to worry about buying one. As I said, Fidelma was nearly as bad as Bentley for causing trouble. I still had to find a hairdresser to get her blasted wig dressed. And find a fur coat for her somewhere. But now we had to provide underwear. Didn't she have a bra? Everyone had a bra. Heather had drawers of them, both old and new which cascaded out if you were looking for a pair of tights or socks. She was one of these hoarders who threw nothing out. Although she'd have to when the baby came. We'd been too busy to think of that, while Heather thought of nothing else. She seemed to have no interest in the play at all. But I suppose all pregnant women are like that.

By coincidence, Dad was working with Fidelma that morning. She was really thick about obeying instructions. Dad would go over the scene with her, patiently explaining things like the blocking, but she wouldn't get it. It drove him crazy. Her character was meant to be really flamboyant, a sort of exaggerated send-up of Mae West. If only she played herself, she'd be OK, but instead she acted flatly, limply, monotonously. It was all wrong.

There was one scene particularly. In it Shirley Temple O'Shea gives out hell to the cast. But she couldn't get the passion into it. She didn't even maintain the same accent — hers was a mixture of Northern Irish and fake Hollywood. I was at the back of the theatre, as she rehearsed that morning.

Shirley: Now, hear this, everybody! I've been waiting around all morning for you bit players to get it together, and if you ask me you're all just a bunch of first-class egotists. That's right! You're forgetting entirely who is the A-number one, tip-top, billing-above-the-title star of this clambake. Well, this is she, and I am telling you, shooting' square from the shoulder and straight from the hips, don't mess with me.

Finally Dad held up a hand. "Fidelma, try and get more aggro into it." He punched the air. "You know the Moore Street traders?"

She nodded sullenly.

"Well, be one! Remember, you're laying down the law. Finish that speech."

She did it in the same emotionless voice.

"Fidelma, hold on!" Dad jumped onto the stage. "Let's take it from the top. I want you to exaggerate for comic effect. Right? You understand? Exaggerate!"

Fidelma reddened. She looked in embarrassment at Oliver Riley who sat with me, gazing adoringly at her. They were definitely an item. Yet she treated him in such an off-hand way.

"Isn't that a lovely frock," he murmured prayerfully.

I nodded.

He was smitten OK. Badly.

For a change Fidelma wasn't wearing her punk gear, but a pretty summer dress which showed up her wonderful tan.

On-stage Dad acted her part, suddenly transforming himself magically into an aggressive has-been Hollywood movie star.

"'Now hear *this*, everybody!' – Try that, Fidelma."

"'Now hear this, everbody,'" she repeated in the same flat way.

Dad was simmering. He acted the part again, shaking a fist. "'Now hear *this*, everybody!'"

"'Now hear this everbody,'" she mumbled.

"Fidelma," Dad's voice was dangerously low, "the word is 'everybody'. Not 'everbody'."

"Eh, it might be better if she says everbody," Luke yelled from the back of the theatre. He must've just come in.

Dad ground his teeth for a minute. "OK, Fidelma, say it Luke's way."

"'Now hear *this*, everybody!'"

"No, no, say it Luke's way!"

"'Everybody hear this now!'" she stammered nervously.

150

God, she was thick.

As Dad put his head in his hands, I asked Ben if he wanted coffee.

Luckily he did.

But back to Fidelma's Wonderbra.

I already had an arrangement to meet her that afternoon. We were to get her a fur coat which she needed for a scene. Again, I'd tried the secondhand places like Oxfam, but could find nothing good enough. So a fur shop had agreed to lend one. Afterwards I'd get her a bra.

After lunch she was waiting outside Bewleys as arranged, heavily made-up in black eyeshadow and eyebrow pencil. It was high summer, so she was wearing no coat over the revealing red sundress. At her feet were two big Marks and Spencers plastic bags, full of shopping.

I glanced at them, wondering why she couldn't afford her own bra? "Hi, Fidelma."

"Thought you'd never come!" she snapped in her Northern accent.

"Sorry. We'll get your fur coat. Then the bra."

She picked up her bags. "Hmm, I need earrings too!"

"You do?"

"Yes, dangling ones."

"I'll see to it," I placated, tearing ahead down the street.

Fidelma's high heels clicked angrily after me. I don't think she liked me very much. She always sort of eyed me up and down, like I was frumpy or something. Or she guessed my virgin status. Maybe it was my jeans and docks. Being the dogsbody, jack-of-all-trades of the production, I sometimes got grubby, or covered in paint. But that was my job — if anyone had a problem, they came to me.

151

"I'm beginning to regret getting involved in this turkey!" She was out of breath.

I stopped. I secretly called our play Dad's last turkey, because he had, and because of his previous ventures. But Fidelma doing it was different. All we needed now was for her to walk out.

"Is anything wrong, Fidelma?" I asked pointedly.

She seized the chance to quiz me. "Has your father directed before?"

"Yes."

She sniffed unbelievingly. "What?"

"Oh, lots of things in London. Mainly at the Royal Court and the Bush."

"I heard he walked off the Gaiety stage."

"That was a long time ago."

Any mention of those years made me queasy. I took off again up the street. I didn't want her saying things about Dad.

She wobbled after me. "Angus is an amateur."

"Yes, but Ivy's famous."

"Back in the twenties?"

"Thirties. And she's getting Angus an Equity card."

She sniffed again – curiously this time. "What about your sister?"

"Equity have agreed to her."

"Has she acted before?" she barked.

"It's her debut."

"Hmm!" Then she sniffed begrudgingly – she had a great range in sniffs. "Doesn't need to act with her looks!"

"No," I called over my shoulder.

"Is Jerry fucking her?"

This made me stop. "She's a bit young."

"Thought I'd check with you."

I rushed on again. "Better check with her."

Did she have her eye on Jerry? Why wasn't she satisfied with Oliver? Or her husband?

She giggled breathily. "Jerry has some balls. Can't say the same for your fella?"

"How can you tell?" I asked outright.

She was matter-of-fact. "The hands."

"Hands?"

"Yeah. Big hands, big cock."

God, I'd never heard that. What was she saying? Jerry had average hands, but was too young for her. So was Shay. She had sex on the brain. But it was something that she considered me to have a claim on him. Maybe she'd seen us lunching together.

We turned into Wicklow Street. The furrier was about halfway down on the right. It was a famous shop and we had to ring a bell to be admitted.

A woman's voice said, "Push the door."

I did. Inside you sank into deep carpets, and along with the mirrors they created a hushed atmosphere of wealth. There didn't seem to be any merchandise in the shop. And no assistants. Only one elegant elderly woman sat at the far end in front of a polished mahogany table.

Feeling awkward and untidy, I went up to her. "Ah, hello."

She had a permanently puzzled expression. She smiled stiffly. "Can I help you, dear?"

"I'm Clare Kelly. I rang . . ."

She obviously didn't expect me.

"It's about a fur coat. We're putting on a play and wondered if you'd lend one as a prop."

The woman frowned. "Did someone promise you?"

"A man I phoned. He said to call in."

153

This baffled her. "Where's your play going on?"

"Talbot Street," I said.

"I didn't know there was a theatre there."

"It's the Pigsty."

Her lip curled. "The Pigsty?"

"Yes, usually The Pigs Litter group use it – you've probably heard of them?"

She shook her head.

"Well, they've rented it to us."

"And what are you putting on?"

"It's – eh – *Tennessee Tierney has not Lived in Vain*. The premier of a new play by Luke Merrill."

"A turkey," Fidelma muttered under her breath.

I felt like killing her.

The woman looked puzzled. "What, dear?"

"It's about a group putting on a play, – I blurted. "Which isn't any good – a disaster, you see. But *our* play's good."

"I see."

"I mean, the play-about-the-play that *we're* putting on. It's good."

"Yes, dear." Then she scanned Fidelma." Is this the actress who'll be wearing the fur?"

"Actor," Fidelma corrected her, with one hand defiantly on her hip.

"We don't usually lend coats," the woman repeated haughtily.

I was crushed. "We'd take great care of it."

The woman shook her head.

"There'd be free tickets to the play," I coaxed. "And a free ad in the programme."

She gave me a funny look. "A free ad in your programme?"

I nodded. "I could give you a whole page."

"Indeed? That would be generous. But we can't risk it, dear. Have you tried a theatrical costumer?"

I shook my head. Was she crazy? That would cost money.

Fidelma had stamped to the door, struggling under her bags. "Who'd wear fur anyway?"

I bit my lip, lingering behind. "You wouldn't make an exception? Just once?"

She shook her head.

"We'd be boycotted by animal rights!" Fidelma hissed from the door.

The woman smiled fleetingly. Had she heard?

"Well, I – I can send the tickets anyway," I said defeatedly. Why didn't Fidelma shut up? "I can't put you in the programme though."

"We'd be boycotted!" came from Fidelma again.

The woman had surely heard that? Red all over, I turned to see her smiling.

"Do you have a business card?" I enquired importantly.

"A business card?"

"With your address?"

She gave me one, still smiling. Now she seemed permanently amused. "I'm sorry we can't help, dear."

I shrugged. "Never mind, I'll try elsewhere."

She looked regretful, calling after me. "Good luck with the play, dear."

"Thanks."

Damn Fidelma. She'd totally alienated the woman. You don't start ranting about animal rights in a fur coat shop. We were out the door when the woman called again, "Wait, dear!"

I went back. Fidelma stood at the door.

The woman was looking at me curiously. "I'd like to

support your efforts, dear. Perhaps . . . I can make an exception in this case. I've just remembered, I have something which might do."

I was all smiles and gestured frantically to Fidelma.

She stamped back with her parcels. "What?"

I pointed to the mirrored wall, as the woman slid back one of them and took out an elegant coat. She held it gingerly up to Fidelma, who grumpily dumped her bags and made to grab it.

But the woman pulled back fussily. "You'll have to wear a cardigan."

When she was getting one, Fidelma muttered crossly in my face, "Does she think my tan's a fake?"

I shrugged weakly. "It looks nice."

"It's not fake!"

"I know."

Was Fidelma going to blow everything now, by being rude to the furrier again? But the woman came back with the cardigan and Fidelma tried it on without comment, preening in front of the mirror. She walked up and down, dripping in furs, like a model prancing the ramp. She looked pretty good.

"Yes," the woman said seriously. "There's just the problem of insurance."

"I'll arrange that," I promised.

She probed further. "The theatre's insured?"

I hadn't a clue, but nodded vigorously.

So she gave me the coat in a huge plastic bag.

Outside I felt triumphant, as if I'd won the Lotto or something. "That was nice of her."

But Fidelma rushed on, screaming, "What are you talking about? No one wears fur anymore!"

"But . . ."

"She couldn't give it away!"

With so many animal rights activists, maybe that was true. Still it was generous of the woman to change her mind. But I was nervous about carrying it around town. What if I was mugged? I was fed up with Fidelma, so gave her a cheque for twenty pounds to buy her own damn bra. Then went for the DART.

It had been a crazy day.

Chapter Fourteen

We couldn't get insurance for the fur coat. And, of course, we hadn't any policy at home to put it on. Grandfather had home owners' insurance, but I was afraid to ask him. So I carried it everywhere in a big plastic bag.

It was strange, in the hottest summer for ten years, to be yanking a fur coat around. But Fidelma couldn't be trusted. She'd only leave it somewhere and then what?

Bentley St Denis was another pain.

Although the best actor in the cast, he continued to clash with Dad. For some reason they irked each other desperately. Bentley sneered all the time. His mobile sometimes went off in the middle of rehearsal and he went into a corner, yelling, "Yaws, yaws, goforrit." Dad asked him repeatedly to switch it off, but he never would. Maybe Bentley wanted to be the director or something. Anyway he constantly challenged Dad, who had christened him "the Menace". I think Dad secretly thought him mad. I could see him reining himself in, placating Bentley about every little whim.

I did my best too.

The cast had to work as a group, communicate psychically with each other. I knew this from my acting classes. Getting on together off-stage was the first essential. The most important thing of all. And on the whole we did. There was a real friendship between some actors and the others had, at least, a growing allegiance to the play.

As well as getting props, I had to make sure that everyone had the right costume. Bentley's clothes for the play were to be everyday – ordinary jeans, etc. Dad said he could wear his own, but his best, not the shabby gear he wore to rehearsals. He came every day in the same grubby white T-shirt, with FUCK THE SYSTEM printed in large black letters on the back. And the same dirty jeans and worn-out tennis shoes. On top of that, he never took a bath.

Katie told me discreetly that the cast objected to being near him and avoided his company outside of rehearsal. She expected me or Dad to do something about this. But how did you tell a grown man to wash?

He'd taken to wearing a baseball cap with S on it. Did that stand for shit? But was the T-shirt legal? You always saw the F-word blanked out in newspapers. Was that because it was illegal to print it?

I imagined all sorts of different scenarios for Bentley.

That maybe he lived in a bedsit without a bath. That he had no money to go to the launderette. They cost a fortune. And he always seemed hungry. He ran into the dressing room ahead of everyone else and wolfed down handfuls of the coffee biscuits and drank all the milk. I had to hide the biscuits and buy extra milk, or there wouldn't be enough for everyone's coffee. It was a puzzle. How could he be so poor? Yet mobiles cost a lot. We hadn't even an answering machine, although Luke had offered to rent one, but Dad said he had no answers.

Bentley was a real puzzle. Had a wealthy family turned its back on him? His accent sounded rich, like Prince Charles with a lisp. And he boasted of having been at Eton. How had someone from there ended up on the dole in Dublin?

As well as the fur coat, I had borrowed a leather jacket and biker's helmet from a motorbike shop for Shay. And I had to buy a red T-shirt for Jerry. Funds were low, so I decided to ask Bentley to wear his best clothes for the play. He was playing a bohemian part anyway.

I picked my moment, mentioning it casually after coffee break one morning. The rest of the cast had gone, and I was washing up. Bentley stood against the wall, in his FUCK THE SYSTEM T-shirt, munching the last of the biscuits and drinking his coffee, while talking into his mobile. "Yaws, yaws. Goforrit. Goforrit."

His hair looked even greasier and he badly needed a shave.

Finally he put his mobile away and contributed his cup. "Here, Clah!"

"Thanks." I ran it under the tap.

It always worried me that we had no hot water to kill the germs, so I boiled a kettle at the end and poured it over.

He stood watching me. "Fancy a drink sometime?"

"What?" God, was he asking me out? It was my one dread – that he'd *like* me. "Thanks – eh, maybe sometime."

He stared sullenly. "What about tonight?"

"Ah, no. I'm busy – props and that. By the way, Bentley, about your gear."

"My gear?"

"Clothes – eh – Dad wants you to wear your best."

He looked at me twitchily over the wire glasses.

"When we open," I explained. "He wants you to look casual, as you do now. Just a bit tidier." I couldn't say "cleaner."

There was another sullen silence.

Nervously I finished the washing up.

He broke it at last. "Are you insulting me, Clah?"

I shook my head vehemently. "No, it's just Dad wants you to look more conventional. "Eh – jeans are fine. Just wear your best."

He looked down at his dirty jeans – his knee was showing through, which was the teenage rage I know, but Bentley was almost middle-aged. "But you're looking at them, Clah."

I was flustered.

"These *are* my best, Clah!"

"I know old jeans are in, but don't you have a better pair?"

"No, Clah, I don't!" He grimaced wryly, scratching his crotch.

I looked away.

He kept scratching.

Did he have to do that? And how come he had no decent clothes? "Don't you have cleaner trainers?"

He folded his arms, grinning defiantly. "No, Clah!"

A complete new outfit would cost a fortune. I plugged in the kettle. "Well, I'll try and borrow some."

This really irked Bentley. He stormed out, shouting, "I'm not wearing anyone else's wags, Clah! If Fidelma got new gear, I jolly well want a measly pair of jeans."

I tried to reason. "But her coat's borrowed, Bentley."

"She got a bwa!"

How did he know that? All I needed was for Dad to be on my back for irritating his best actor. The relationship between them was strained enough.

"Bentley!" I pleaded. "Come back!"

He didn't.

"Please!"

He still didn't. Was he insulted because I wouldn't have a drink with him? But he gave me the creeps. I couldn't go out

161

with him. Not even for Dad's play. That would be the ultimate sacrifice.

When I told Dad that evening that Bentley wanted new clothes, he groaned, without looking up from the evening paper. "What does he think we are? The Vincent de Paul?"

I hated actors – some, anyway. I wouldn't include Ivy or Shay. Or Oliver. "What'll I do?"

Dad sighed. "Be firm, Clare."

"But Dad –"

He rustled his newspaper irritably. "Say *no*!"

"He knows about Fidelma's bra."

Dad laughed shortly. "Does he want one too?"

I didn't answer. Why did Dad dump everything on me? I was getting fed up. Was I a football to be kicked by all? I was eighteen, and Bentley was about thirty-five. How could I be firm with him? He was an absolute spacer.

Then Dad said grumpily, "OK. If the Iron Maiden got a bra, I suppose he can get jeans – in Dunnes though!"

"I can't take a grown man shopping."

Dad frowned over his paper. "It's your job, Clare."

The next day after rehearsal we went into Dunnes in Talbot Street. I thought Bentley'd be grateful for a new outfit – anything would look better than his penurious rags. I pointed to a rail of blue denims. "Why don't you try on a pair?"

But Bentley looked scornfully at them. "Clah, I can't wah those."

I was taken aback. "What's wrong with them?"

"They're muck, Clah. Muck." He walked to the next rail in a huff.

I looked at the jeans. They seemed OK. "But they're good quality."

He came back. "Look at the stitching, Clah?"

The stitching? He was a right one to talk about stitching. "But Dad wears Dunnes."

It was the wrong thing to say. Mention of my father set him into a rage, and he stormed out of the shop, screaming at the top of his lungs, "I'm not wearing muck! You can tell him that!"

I caught him in the street. "Wait, Bentley, please!"

He swung round. "I'm sick of the whole thing."

"But Bentley —"

"I'm pulling out."

"You're the best actor!"

He softened at this.

"The play depends on you," I added.

He sniffed. "Did your Dad say that?"

I nodded vehemently. "He's *always* saying that."

Actually Dad had still never commented on the actors to me.

"Hmm . . ." He stood glaring down at me over his glasses, with folded arms. "It's Levi's, or nothing, Clah. OK?"

"OK."

"*New* Levi's, understand?"

"Yes, new Levi's."

For God's sake. Everyone knew Irish Levi's were about forty pounds. What would Dad say? I knew he was in the Pigsty, rehearsing Fidelma who could still never get the blocking. It'd be awkward asking him in front of so many people. Maybe I could ring him? If I pretended to go to the Ladies in a pub, I could phone Dad before he went home.

There was a Levi's jean store across the street. I told

163

Bentley to go there and pick out a pair, while I looked for a phone booth.

Have you ever noticed that there are only card phones if you have the money and only coin phones if you have the card. I had a card but there were no card phones.

As I walked back along the street, there was a man staring at the Pigsty. I'd seen him before. It was Mr Connors – Shay's da.

I'd know his bald head anywhere. What was he doing there?

He looked suspicious.

I ducked into a pub at the end of the street.

It was a dark northside pub. Old men stared morosely into their afternoon beer. You could hardly see, but finally I found the phone in the corner – a new-fangled type in which you had to put 30p, after you dialled the number. I put the money in first and lost it.

I asked the barman for more change. "Could you give me a 20p bit?"

He had a red swollen face and was sullenly wiping the counter top. "Whatja want it for?"

I was taken aback. "The phone."

"Did I say yeh could use it?"

"Eh, no." There was drink on his breath.

"Yeh didn't ask!"

"Sorry."

"I wouldn't go into yer house and use yer phone without asking."

What was he talking about? "But this is a public house."

His bloodshot eyes bulged. "What?"

I felt myself go beetroot. "A public house is open to the public."

"It is not!"

"It isn't?" I was mortified. People were looking.

"No!"

"I could bring a dead body in here." Grandfather had told me a public house couldn't refuse the public, even if dead.

His eyes nearly popped out of his face. "You could not! And you can get out now!"

I fled.

Damn him, anyway. Who would have thought a person could act like that over a phone call? It must've been something about my face. Did I look dishonest?

I went back up the street to the Levi's shop. Mr Connors was gone, but Bentley was in the shop, already dressed in a complete new outfit – expensive 501s and a new red check shirt. He'd also picked out a new pair of Nikes.

He paraded in front of me. "What do you think, Clah?"

I just looked at him. I was too shaken by the barman to say anything.

"Will I do, Clah?"

I nodded weakly.

The bill came to over a hundred pounds.

I told Dad nervously after dinner that evening.

He had a fit. "You spent what?"

"A hundred pounds."

He paled. "Clare . . ."

"Bentley refused to wear anything from Dunnes."

"He what! Well . . . !" Then Dad began ranting and raving. "Why did I cast that prick! We'll have to sell twenty seats to pay for those, Clare!"

He banged the table with his fist.

Heather was knitting furiously. She was big now and rows

165

were bad for the baby, still she challenged him. "Don't shout, Dan!"

"I will shout!"

He hovered over her, clenching his fists.

Oh, God. He'd hit her in a minute. Why were men like leopards who never changed their spots? He was still violent — a bully.

I began to cry.

Katie paled in fear.

"Now see what you've done!" Heather lumbered over and put her arms around me. "Clare, darling. Don't mind him."

But Dad wouldn't stop yelling. "We can't afford to outfit the cast!"

"I couldn't help it!" I sobbed. "He bought them while I was trying to phone you!"

"Leave her alone, Dan!" Heather shouted again.

I could see he was holding himself in. He stood there, taut, ready to leap. "She shouldn't have paid for them!"

Then he ran out, banging the door.

Heather lumbered after him.

They shouted at each other in the garden.

I went to bed in tears. I was mad with myself for being so unassertive. First with the mad barman. Then with Bentley. It was all a cod — the assistant director shit. I was a dogsbody, a whipping girl. My job consisted of four things: getting coffee, getting props, getting things clean, and getting told off.

Katie followed me. She sat on the squeaky bed. "Will I ring the ISPCA?"

I pulled the duvet over my head. "It's the ISPCC."

"Well, them, then."

"No. I'm not a child."

"*Women's Aid* then. It's emotional abuse."

166

"Oh, stop exaggerating."

A schoolfriend of Katie's had once rung Childline, and so she'd always wanted to do the same. But she wasn't exaggerating – I only said that to keep the peace. I'd had it with the whole thing too. After all I'd done, Dad wasn't even grateful. Since the rehearsal fuss, he treated Katie with kid gloves. I was picked on for the least thing. Why had Heather put up with him all those years? She was an idiot to follow him around the way she did. He hadn't changed at all. He didn't like her going for a walk by herself. He even resented her pathetic night classes. He'd always have a violent streak. He was no better than Shay's da. The thought of Shay brought on tears. I wanted to be his girlfriend. But he'd *never* care for me. It was madness to hope for any happiness in life. From men anyway. Katie and Jerry took every opportunity to be alone together. But Shay had never even touched me. Not ever. What could be wrong with me?

"'How do you make a sandwich spread?'" Katie hugged her knees. She was wearing my black leggings. And smoking.

I didn't answer.

"Come on, guess!"

"I dunno."

"'By sitting on it'!"

She collapsed back in giggles.

I had to smile.

"Try this one: 'When was Napoleon born?'

I shrugged. "Dunno."

"'On his birthday!'

I smiled again. "Is that Dad's cigarette?"

She nodded.

"Hmm . . . Just don't steal Luke's."

"OK. Try this one – 'What did the candle say to the other candle?'"

I sighed, she never gave up. "Wouldn't have a clue."

"'Are you going out tonight?'"

This transported her again. Finally she stopped laughing at her own idiotic joke. "Jerry and I are off to a disco. Come with us."

I shook my head.

"Ah, come on!"

"No." I'd only been to a couple of discos. Maybe that was my whole problem. But I couldn't stand dancing. It was traumatic, jumping around.

I lay there, while Katie got dressed.

"Can I wear your blue top?" she begged.

"OK. But take care of it." She'd burnt a cigarette hole in my other one. There were holes in several of my things from her carelessness. All the others were stretched out of shape. But I didn't care any more.

Katie finally left. After a bit, Heather came in. "Dad's sorry, darling."

She looked so tired and pregnant that I nodded. Then tears came – I couldn't help it.

She held me in her arms. "Clare, darling. He knows it's not your fault."

I kept crying. For years I'd missed her so much.

"Clare –"

Finally I got control of myself. "I thought it'd be so great when you guys came back."

She pushed my hair out of my face.. "We are back and it is great. But you have your life, darling."

I wanted a life with them. But there was no way I could explain that. The open road was before me, but I wanted to find the briary lane back to my childhood. That I'd lost because of my parents. Now they were beginning all over again.

I put my hand on her tummy. "What's it feel like?"

"It's tiring, but exciting." Her hair roots had grown out dark. Pregnancy must be ageing, because she seemed to have more wrinkles etched around her eyes. But Heather was the eternal optimist.

"You love Dad a lot, don't you?"

She nodded. "I know it seems like I put him first – before you girls."

We'd never really talked about it. But it was exactly what I did think. Still I didn't blame her. Although Katie did. For years she'd been very angry.

"I couldn't let him go, darling. You'll understand some day."

"I do understand." Why had Dad never turned into Mr Right? It wasn't fair on Heather. She loved him so much. Then I blurted, "I think I'm in love."

Heather looked shocked. "Well . . . I'm used to Katie's flings. I know I'll have to let her go. But you?"

I reddened. "Yeah."

It was like balm, that she didn't want to let me go. I could stay young for a bit longer.

"Who is it?" she asked.

"Shay."

Heather blinked unbelievingly. "Well, he seems a nice boy."

"His father hits him. He's a criminal. I saw him in Talbot Street today."

"It's a public street."

"But he was staring up at the theatre. He hates Shay."

"Poor boy."

Tears filled my eyes. "I like him so much."

Heather looked at me sadly. "Love is long, darling. And youth is short."

"What do you mean?"

"You're too young to be serious."

"Don't worry. He hasn't noticed me.".

"You'll get into Trinity and everything will be fine," she went on.

"I won't get into the Beckett Centre."

"You're being negative, Clare."

I wasn't so sure.

Then she went to make me coffee.

Luke brought it in.

He wore his uniform white Aran sweater, which showed up his tan. Even in our wonderful summer, he was always cold. He looked down on me with his kind blue eyes. "Hi, Clare."

"Hi." I turned to the wall.

He put down his cup and plonked on my bed. "Wanna talk?"

"OK."

I loved his coffee, but was embarrassed to be seen with red eyes. Heather must have told him about the hideous row, because he wasn't in when it happened. Dad wouldn't have made such a show of himself with him around, which is one argument for having visitors. Although Luke was more of a lodger now – a family member really.

He ran his hand through his thick unruly hair. Then sipped his coffee. It was probably laced with Bourbon, as usual. I kept stopping myself from saying we had glasses – we weren't that bad. But he was doing it for Dad. It was kind of him to hide his drinking, considering Dad's problems – but that was Luke. How was Dad an alcoholic, but not him?

He said nothing at first. Just looked concerned. He was non-judgmental. It was the most noticeable thing about him — he saw things from all angles. Like a lawyer or some terribly wise, fair person. He was a Libra, which made me think there was definitely something in Heather's astrology, because Libras are just like Luke.

At last he said, "Clare, the play wouldn't be possible without you."

I stared into my coffee. "It would."

He shook his head. "Wouldn't."

I laughed sarcastically. "Dad'd find someone else to kick around."

Luke ran his hands through his thick hair. "Your Dad's had a lot of stress."

I caught my breath. "He's caused a lot too."

"He's a very tense person, Clare."

I liked Luke so much. But I was sick of hearing about Dad's problems. "Because of Vietnam?"

Luke was puzzled. "Vietnam?"

"Yeah, it made Dad into an alcoholic."

"Hmm." Luke took out his cigarettes. "Mind if I smoke?"

"No." What else could I say?

Luke lit up thoughtfully. "Well, we were both drafted for Vietnam —"

"You saw combat and that?"

Luke smiled. "A lot of people in the army never see combat, Clare."

I was puzzled. "But Dad killed people?"

Luke laughed. "Who told you that?"

I sat up. "That's why he drank. Heather said."

"I don't know why she said that. Your dad and I were paper pushers. I worked in a military hospital and your dad was a typist."

I laughed out loud. "A typist?"

He nodded. "We never got near the fighting."

God. After all Dad's stories.

There was a long silence.

"Well, don't tell, Heather," I said finally. "She thinks Vietnam caused his drinking."

Luke inhaled deeply. Wreaths of smoke hid his face.

"Why did he tell Heather that?" I asked after a second.

He shrugged. "We all try to excuse our actions."

I stared at the cracked ceiling. So it was all a myth? Dad was a typist. When I'd thought of him in bunkers, or maybe in cages like that scary film *The Deerhunter*.

Then Luke said. "You and Shay seem thick, Clare?"

I nodded. Had Heather told him? It was unlike her to repeat a confidence. No, Luke had seen Shay and me walking off together at lunch. Maybe he'd advise me. "Nothing ever happens. Between us."

A look of bafflement crossed his face. "Sweetheart –"

"I want to be a sexy person."

He frowned, looking down at the bedcover. "You are sexy, Clare. Brains are just as important as beauty."

Funny I could talk to him more easily than to either of my parents. If I wasn't in love with Shay, I'd be in love with Luke. But he wouldn't notice me either.

He tried to say something which wouldn't come out. Instead he went to the door. "Now, will you put this upset behind you?"

I nodded, thinking of Shay and Ivy, Jerry and Katie, how much they all wanted the play to succeed. Everyone wasn't like Bentley or Fidelma. Or Dad.

After Luke left, I lay there thinking of all the stuff Dad had told us about his youth. How he'd just escaped his southern family to go to College. Then he'd been drafted against his will and how it ruined his whole life. But he'd just been a boring typist. I never even saw him typing now. It was pathetic.

About eleven o'clock, he knocked on my door. "Clare."

I pretended to be asleep.

He came in and sat wearily on the bed. "I'm sorry, pumpkin."

I wouldn't look at him.

"Clare . . . ?" He had that blank, innocent look.

"What?"

"Guess I've really screwed up this time, eh?"

He'd been out and was still wearing his tweed jacket. I used to think we had the handsomest father in the school. But no one ever saw him. He never came to Parents' Day. Or anywhere near the place.

He rubbed the back of his neck. "Usually costumes are supplied to actors, but in our case, funds are low."

I said nothing.

"Bentley took advantage of you."

I still didn't answer.

"I never thanked you for all you've done."

I started crying again. It was just like long ago. He'd do awful things and then expect you to feel sorry for him.

He looked miserable. "Come on, Clare. Stop this."

I couldn't.

He touched my arm. "You've no idea how much I depend on you."

I furiously wiped my eyes. "But you yelled."

He looked sad. "Sorry."

"You were just like . . . before." The thought of those terrible years brought on more tears, but I held them back. "Luke said you never killed people."

173

He raised his eyebrows. "I should hope not!"

"But you said you were ordered to – in Vietnam."

Dad shook his head adamantly. "I don't think I ever said that, pumpkin. I was drafted by the army. The army killed people. I was a pacifist, but I didn't have the courage to desert. Other people did. I was young and stupid. I started drinking heavily. I might've escaped alcoholism in a different situation." He shrugged resignedly. "But probably not."

I didn't know what to say.

He eventually broke the silence. "I thought we'd agreed to leave all that, Clare."

I couldn't answer. I was still afraid I'd cry.

He sighed wearily. "'Children begin by loving their parents, after a time they judge them; rarely, if ever, do they forgive them.'"

"Who said that?"

"Oscar Wilde."

"He was right."

"The past's dead, pumpkin. The future matters – the play."

Dad had such faith, it was pathetic.

"The whole project would collapse without you," he went on.

He did need me. "That's what Luke said."

"You don't believe me?"

Why hadn't he let me act?

"I'd prefer to be acting."

He gave me a long sad look, then slowly shook his head. "Clare, your grades are always so good."

"What's that got to do with it?"

"I want something better for you. Not acting."

I couldn't believe what he was saying. His whole life had been dedicated to the arts.

174

"The theatre's too hard, pumpkin."

I sat up. "But you *love* the theatre."

He nodded slowly. "When this is over, we'll take a trip to London. We'll see some plays. Just you and me."

That's if we weren't in debtors' prison.

"OK?"

"OK."

It'd never happen. He was always promising things. But I let him hug me.

Chapter Fifteen

Even if it made his behaviour less forgivable, I was glad my dad hadn't killed anyone. The Kellys had no blood on their hands. I didn't have to avoid looking a Vietnamese in the eye, if I ever met one. But it was a puzzle. He'd told heroic stories all these years. Now he said we'd just imagined he played a part in the adventures. His stories weren't about him, but about other men he'd known. He'd never staked out a village, and the only time he'd crawled on his belly was in boot camp in Alabama. Somewhere the wires had got crossed. With Heather too.

It was a puzzle, but there was no time to think any more about it. I put the row behind me, and carried on with my job. I even smiled at Bentley, complimenting him on his new clothes. Thank God, he had no idea what had happened with Dad. We were a family again, an extended family including the cast, putting on a play. That left no room for personal grievances.

As the day of reckoning drew nearer, a magic thing happened. The cast got really fond of each other. Except for Bentley they had united into a group, all working for the common good. It was magic. Even people who had clashed earlier like Ivy and Angus became like lovers. Even Fidelma had changed – sort of. She invited Jerry to tea at her house. He couldn't go and asked me to phone and explain. I did and she understood. She was actually nice about it, saying rather sadly, "Thanks for telling me, Clare."

I was puzzled. Why hadn't Jerry gone?

Why ask him and not the others?

Then it hit me – she liked Jerry. It was a summer of love. There was more drama offstage than on. The chain was getting bigger: Aunt Brigid liked Oliver who liked Fidelma who liked Jerry who liked Katie. Not to mention Ivy's secret love. Or mine.

Only Bentley remained an outsider. He asked me out again, and sulked because I still refused. Even in his new clothes he didn't attract me. He never would. He was a creep. Always griping about something – the blocking, the lighting, the play itself. About two days before opening night, he caused another bad row.

Luke wanted to make a small change in the script. Dad agreed. He told the cast at rehearsal that day.

Everyone was amenable – everyone but Bentley.

"I can't change now!" he shouted.

Dad paled. "You can and you will!"

"I will not! It's too late!"

"It's a couple of words." Dad shook his fist in rage.

Oh, God.

Then Bentley jumped off the stage, and ran up the aisle yelling. "I won't! I won't!"

"Get your ass back here!" Dad shouted at the top of his lungs.

In a minute he'd lose it. He'd fly into an appalling rage and chase after Bentley.

I put my head in my hands. It was a case of men at work.

177

The other actors stared in dismay, as Bentley tore out of the theatre.

Dad looked ready to kill. "Come back here, sonny!"

Bentley turned at the lobby door. "No, I'm going home! I utterly object to last minute changes!"

"Right! You're fired!" Dad screamed. "And keep *goingforrit* till you get to the river. Then jump in!"

Bentley ran out, banging the doors.

Everyone quaked.

It took Luke about a half-an-hour to talk Bentley into coming back. Luke had the ability to soothe and make things right. He was another peacemaker. Blessed be Luke. Blessed be all the peacemakers, for they shall save the theatre. My first, my last, my only love – except for Shay. And, of course, Katie and Heather and Dad – sometimes. And Ivy – always.

"Naughty, Bentley!" Ivy scolded later that day and he just laughed at her.

Weird. He didn't get annoyed with her.

Ivy was a mother figure and constantly rallied the cast, bringing in homemade cakes for rehearsal hunger. I knew how poor she was. Yet she was always doing things for people. She found a hairdresser for Fidelma's wig and lent her a pair of dangling earrings.

But, close to opening, she too had an attack of nerves.

It happened like this: Dad wanted a basically bare stage with a white half-drawn curtain at the back – to indicate a rehearsal space, a rehearsal was after all the main plot of our play. But Ivy wanted the curtain gone. And, when Dad refused to remove it, had a tantrum.

I couldn't believe it.

"No, Mr Kelly," she waved a hand flamboyantly, "I absolutely insist that you remove that horrible sheet."

"The curtain stays, Ivy," Dad said flatly.

"In that case, I go." She swept regally up the aisle.

Angus looked after her from under his hooded lids. All the other actors stood there. No one else said anything in support of her – except Aunt Brigid.

"Dan, it's hideous," she grumped. "I agree with the Countess."

He ignored her, so she hobbled out after Ivy.

Dad went backstage.

Was Ivy really leaving? This woman had been such an inspiration to me.

Dad did nothing to stop her. Couldn't he humour her? Say something, anything to stop her going? She had always been so helpful. She was so lovely. A diva to die for. One word from him and she'd come back.

But he didn't.

I stood there, not knowing what to do.

Then I ran up the aisle after her. "Ivy, wait!"

She turned, relieved but still firm. "I'm sorry, Clare. I've put up with everything up to this, but I cannot abide that curtain."

"I don't like it either," Aunt Brigid parroted. "She's absolutely right, Clare!"

The two of them were so vulnerable.

God, what was I to do? The curtain was pretty awful, but Dad was the director. It was the director's job to decide on the set. The costumes, the props. Where was Luke? No sign of him.

Ivy was in the lobby, tearfully pulling on long white gloves. "I'm going home to my garden!"

"You can't leave!" I gently took her arm. "Please come back. I'll work on Dad."

She considered this. "You will? Well . . ."

"I promise." I hugged her.

"For your sake, Clare." Her voice trembled. "Yours alone."

Ivy came back.

The curtain stayed.

Two days before opening and things were going well – the cast knew their lines. Even Ivy seemed to. I had lent her Katie's Walkman, but she didn't seem to need it. And Fidelma – well she sort of knew them. The blocking was still a bit vague to her and she might as easily wind up on stage right as stage left.

"No one will notice," said Oliver, typically calm and kind.

We'd had one rehearsal without books which went well. There were one or two rough spots, but Dad was working on them.

The invitations to critics were sent out. Flyers were left around all the Dublin hotels, personally and professionally by me. Several hotel porters had promised to send customers. The theatre was painted, and the props all ready. Luke was doing the lights. Aunt Brigid was selling tickets in the booth. I was to be backstage.

Then something terrible happened.

We had a break-in.

The morning before our first preview night, Dad, Luke and I arrived at the Pigsty to find that the door had been forced open.

The place was ransacked.

We just stood there in shock. Some lunatic had taken an axe to the stage. Whoever it was had really gone to work. What forces were we grappling with? I remembered that boy on the Bray beach, furiously building his sandcastle. But finally losing it to the force of the waves. Our castle had almost been built. Now it was badly battered.

Dad was in despair. "Shit! I don't believe it!"

It was too much. After all the trouble getting the money to start. The weeks of rehearsal. Then Bentley and Fidelma's tantrums. Now this. Would we be able to stage the play? Or would we have to cancel the whole damn thing at the very last minute?

Luke looked upward to the ceiling. "The roof window's broken."

The intruders had got in from a roof window, battering it completely. There was glass all over the place. They must have left through the front lobby.

We were all shaken.

And puzzled.

Dad especially. "But what the hell did they want?"

OK, there was the Dublin drug problem – the heroin addicts who needed money to feed their habit. But Talbot Street wasn't a particularly bad area. Anywhere across the river in North Dublin was rougher than anywhere on the south side. But why rob an unimportant fringe theatre? The play hadn't even opened yet, and even if it had, the box office takings wouldn't be left overnight.

Then I noticed. "The props are gone."

"What?" the men said together.

I pointed to a corner of the stage. "They were there!"

Dad ran backstage, wailing, "I don't believe this!"

The props for Katie's character were usually left on-stage, as there was no room backstage. But they were all definitely gone – the deer's head, the bull fiddle, the iron cauldron, even Ivy's picnic basket.

Gone.

All gone.

It was weird. Who'd sabotaged our turkey? The bird that

was to lay our golden egg? Dublin was a poor place, but who'd want useless stuff like that? Thieves usually went for TV video recorders.

Dad punched the air. "Shit!"

Luke flattened his wild hair calmly. "The place must be insured, Dan."

"Fat lot of good!" Dad roared. "Shit!"

Finally the owners came in. They immediately called the guards who took fingerprints and talked to Dad and Luke. Then the carpenters and glaziers were phoned. Luke was right – the theatre owners had insurance, but only for the building, not goods. Although they promised to put the theatre quickly to rights, we couldn't claim anything for our props.

What now?

The bull fiddle was the only valuable thing. But I'd no idea how much it was worth. Although more or less useless, some of the other props were antiques. Besides being needed for our play, they belonged to others. How were we to replace them?

Shay and Jerry had come in. They were meant to rehearse a scene with Dad that morning and now they stood around mournfully. I don't know where Katie was. Probably still sleeping.

Shay rubbed his bristly face with a hand – a habit of his, muttering, "Jaysus . . . Ah, for fuck's sake."

Dad snapped, "There'll be no rehearsals today, son."

Jerry looked even more mournful. He stared at the damage through his shades. There was something helpless in his burliness.

Shay set about examining everything carefully, while muttering the F-word under his breath.

"This is it!" Dad wailed. "We can't go on without props."

"I'll get more," I said. "The antique shop was really nice."

"They're not going to be too nice now!" Dad was inconsolable.

Shay didn't speak. He was too busy looking at the broken roof window, the axed stage, the glass, everything. Finally he peered at the broken door. Then quietly went over to Dad. "It's a fuckin' inside job."

Dad's eyebrows shot up. "What?"

"It's fuckin' someone from the play."

Dad didn't seem able to take that in.

"An inside fuckin' job," Shay persisted. "Someone fuckin' knew what they were fuckin' lookin' fer."

"They wanted our props?" Dad's eyebrows were raised. "Oh, come on!" He laughed hysterically.

Shay nodded knowingly.

Dad was unconvinced. "But why?"

"Antiques are valuable," Jerry said in his Cork sing-song. "A bull fiddle could bring in a pretty penny now."

"Sabotage," Shay announced flatly. "Someone hates us!"

Dad gaped in disbelief. Who hated us? Could we get more props in one day? Despite what I'd said to Dad, I was afraid to go back to the antique shop and tell them what had happened. Luckily the fur coat was safe, as I still carried it with me everywhere in the big plastic bag. That was probably the most valuable item of all.

Shay jerked his head at me. "Come on, Clare! Jerry!"

The boys made for the door and I obediently followed, waving to a puzzled Dad and Luke.

"We'll be back!" I called. "Mind the coat!"

Shay set off, running up Talbot Street. I ran after him, not knowing why. It was something to do, and I was getting away from Dad's moods. The street buzzed with crowds and hawkers

183

selling illegal cigarettes. Jerry, who was heavier, lumbered after us. We ran up O'Connell Street and across the bridge.

"Tha' shit lives in Synge Street," Shay panted.

I just about kept up. "What shit?"

"Sin Denis!"

I was out of breath. "Sin Denis? You mean Bentley?"

"Yeah, he lives near the plannin' place, right?"

"What planning place?"

"The family plannin' place. In Synge Street."

I'd heard of the IFPA. Unfortunately, as yet, I'd had no need of their services. "You go there for contraceptives?"

Shay nodded. "For me ma."

"Your ma?" Maybe I should've gone there for Heather. But I couldn't think about that now. "But what shit lives there?"

"That fuckin' maggot!"

"What fucking maggot?"

"That fuckin' Bentley Sin Denis creep. He asked me round once."

Then I got it. "You think he committed the robbery?"

"I'm fuckin' sure he did."

"But you need evidence, proof, clues, fingerprints, stuff like that."

Shay pointed to his heart. "I got all the fuckin' clues here."

What was he talking about?

Dublin was a permanent rush-hour. The traffic was always chaotic. Carbon monoxide fumes nearly choked you. It was gradually eating away the stone in Trinity College and the Bank of Ireland. They were meant to be doing something about the traffic, but it just got worse. Maybe when the buildings fell down, they'd do something. Or all the asthmatics like Heather died.

We were almost killed at the Trinity lights. Brakes shrieked as Shay rushed in front of a car. The driver glared and honked. But Shay was unfazed.

Waiting for the green man, he muttered. "I get fuckin' hunches, Clare."

"Well, hunches aren't good enough. You need proof."

The lights changed as Jerry caught us.

Shay charged on. "I'll get fuckin' proof."

We ran around College Green and all the way up South Great George's Street, breathing in traffic fumes, until we got to Kelly's Corner. Then we passed the old grey church and turned into Synge Street where we rang Bentley's bell. The house opposite had a plaque, saying George Bernard Shaw had lived there. I remembered what Ivy had said about there being two tragedies in life – one not getting what you want; the other to get it. Was the play going to fall through now?

We waited.

No one came.

"He's left!" Shay jabbed another bell.

"But Shay?" I was getting nervous. This was crazy. What was he planning to do? Accuse Bentley of theft? He was about half his size. "Let's not do this."

He rang the bell again. "We have to get into that fuckin' room, Clare! The props are in there!"

Jerry was hesitant too. He had a countryman's caution. He ruffled his helmet of black hair "Arra now, I don't think we should."

But Shay was determined. "Look, you fuckin' stay outside and keep watch. OK. You see that fuckin' gobshite, you distract him, OK?"

"OK." Jerry waited nerdily in the street. He looked like some sort of spy in his sunglasses. But he was so gentle, I didn't see him in that role. In a way Katie had got her desire, in finding someone who resembled Liam Gallagher. Jerry was "boobsolutely abuful," a boob, a babe. No wonder Fidelma wanted him.

We rang the bell again.

Finally an old lady in a dressing gown and slippers answered it. She had rouge-daubed cheeks and a hairnet over curlers. She peered round the big door. "Can I help you?" Her accent was genteel.

Shay put on a middle-class accent. "Eh – we're friends of Bentley St Denis."

The old woman smiled faintly. "Such a nice young man."

"He's expectin' us, but he's out. Can we wait in his flat?"

The old woman hesitated. "Well – I do have a key . . ."

Shay pushed the door. "Great."

"I can't go in there while he's out," she added worriedly.

"Ah, it'll be OK," Shay insisted.

She frowned, muttering something inwardly. "You're sure he's out?"

Shay nodded. She tried the bell herself.

No answer again.

"Well . . ." The woman still looked uncertain.

But Shay pushed her. "We're just off the boat from England. If we don't sleep, we'll drop somewhere."

He did a staggering act.

This seemed to worry her. "Well, if you're sure it's all right?"

We nodded emphatically. "We're expected. He told us to wait."

She tried the bell for a second time, but again no answer.

"Well, I do have a key." She padded off down the corridor. "And you children look tired."

Miraculously, we were allowed into Bentley's bedsit. It was

at the top of a grim stairway with an old greasy carpet and dank peeling wallpaper.

"You'll be able to find everything you want?" The old lady opened his door on the first landing.

"Yes, thank you." I closed it gently.

There was a sink in one corner and a small electric grill in the other. The bed was unmade and there were cups half full of cold coffee everywhere. There was a torn poster of Kenneth Branagh as Henry V on the wall. Everything was so bleak and untidy. Bentley was always *goingforrit*. Why hadn't he ever got anywhere?

Shay stood in the middle of the room. "The props must be fuckin' some place."

He yanked open a big wardrobe.

Inside was a bag of dirty laundry.

No props.

But there was an axe — a sort of small hatchet for chopping wood.

Shay took it out. "What'd I tell ya?"

"Be careful," I said.

"What?"

"Fingerprints!"

He put it down quickly. "Yeah, we need fuckin' evidence."

I was sceptical. "There's a fireplace. Maybe he chops wood."

Dubliners did in winter. Despite central heating, the city was full of miserable bedsitters heated with fireplaces like this. The axe was in the wardrobe because he didn't need it in summer. It proved nothing. Bentley still sulked with me. Some days he didn't address me at all. But he seemed committed to the play and, despite being so difficult, was acting well. Had he

187

smashed everything up? On a mad whim? At the eleventh hour? If so, what could be his motive?

I looked at Shay. "There's no proof."

"Oh, yeah?" He pointed again to the axe. "Well, what's he doing with this?"

"I told you, it's for wood."

Bentley was mad, but not that mad. Hell hath no fury like a man scorned, but I wasn't a motive. I couldn't be. We'd duped a poor old woman to get in here. The sooner we left the better.

Chapter Sixteen

The show must go on.

And ours did.

I persuaded Shay not to accuse Bentley. It would finish us, if he was innocent and pulled out in a huff. Repairs on the stage were hastily carried out. And the window replaced. The Pigsty was put back together like Humpty Dumpty.

Dad gradually recovered from the shock.

We scraped up more props – a cello from Oliver Riley's daughter to replace the bull fiddle, a birdcage from a friend of Ivy's and another deer's head from the antique shop in Francis Street. They were understanding and said that it didn't matter too much if the original one didn't turn up, as they were going out of that line anyway. They were fantastic people. But thank God for the animal rights movement. We now only had to think about refunding the music academy for the bull fiddle. I didn't know what to do about that, so for the moment shelved it.

The press invites had gone out, and the critics had confirmed that they were coming.

Our first night came, like everything else in life. Everything looked great. The show was advertised in the *Evening Herald*.

I'd brought flowers from grandfather's garden and arranged them in the lobby. Dad stood nervously at the back of the theatre. Luke disappeared into the lights box. Aunt Brigid was in the ticket booth ready for the hordes of customers.

A few trickled in.

I gave up peeping through the curtains and waited with the actors in the cramped dressing-room. They huddled silently, tense but noble, like Sidney Carton awaiting execution. There was a sense of dedication, of common cause. Even Fidelma was quiet and sat murmuring – prayers, maybe? Bentley also sat with his eyes closed. He looked tidy in his expensive new gear and had actually shampooed his ponytail.

Opening his eyes suddenly, he caught my stare.

.I reddened. "Good luck, Bentley."

He nodded grumpily and went back to his meditation.

Had he stolen the props and ransacked the theatre? Despite Shay's theories, there was definitely no proof. Bentley was cracked OK, but not that cracked. He was his normal dour self now. The chopping axe was only circumstantial evidence. Thank God his landlady hadn't mentioned our stupid visit to his place. Why had I gone along with Shay's mad idea?

Katie was chain-smoking in the corner. She was a knockout in black leggings and a white shirt.

"Break a leg," I whispered, giving her a little hug.

She was puzzled. "Eh, what?"

"Break a leg – it means, 'good luck.'"

"Oh . . ." She pulled on her fag. "I'm dreading it."

"You'll be fine."

Her eyes widened. "Will I?"

"Yeah, you were great at the rehearsals. Wasn't she, Jerry?"

He was meditating in the far corner. Now he looked over adoringly. He was a love-sick swain. "She was fab."

190

I loved my sister and, more than anything, wanted her success. I was ashamed of my envy. I'd been obsessed by the green eye of the little yellow god. You didn't get all the gumdrops in life, as Dad always said. It was lucky that no one could read your thoughts – I'd wanted to kill her.

Ivy sat doing her breathing exercises under a big straw hat. It was antediluvian, like the rest of her outfit. In case her memory failed, her scenes were written out in big letters and pinned to the inside of the picnic basket. She was to open it on her entrance. But it was back-up. She knew her lines. She only had two scenes and hopefully she'd remember them.

"Breathe deeply, darling," she whispered to my sister now.

Katie did.

"And don't prevent others!" Bentley batted the air neurotically. "Smoke's bad for my voice."

God, he was at it again.

Katie stubbed out her cigarette. "Sorry, Bentley."

"Naughty, Bentley!" Ivy wagged a finger. "You're upsetting the child."

As he pouted, she instructed my sister, "Now straighten your shoulders, breathe, hold for ten . . ."

I left them to it, peeping from behind the stage curtain to the theatre.

More people had come. Amazingly Grandfather sat with Heather in the front row. He wore a jaunty cravat, but had his usual stiff expression. She looked more pregnant now, and very happy. It was weird to see them together. Shay's ma was beside them. She'd had her hair permed into tight little yellow curls and wore a white summer cardigan. The rest of the small house was mainly filled with complimentaries – the press, theatre people, Luke's redheaded girlfriend and Dad's friends. I tried to discern who was a critic and who not. I recognised the man from *The Irish Times,* and there was a young woman from the *Herald* beside him. There were a couple of empty benches at the back.

But at least we had an audience. The play existed.

The curtain went up.

Everyone was quiet.

I watched from the wings as Bentley opened strongly with his monologue. He was always good and performed reliably now. There was relaxed laughter in the house at Luke's jokes.

Oliver came on as T Boyle. Then the young people. Then the two geriatrics. The audience laughed again at Shay's running commentary on their entrance:

> They're almost here, outside, clutchin' the area
> railings, inching along. They're at the door, they're
> through the door . . .

Ivy and Angus came on. More Laughter.

We were on our way.

Our turkey was going to fly.

The house was completely relaxed. Then came the bit where Bentley gets the chair.

Ivy dried.

Completely.

Hell, why didn't she open the picnic basket?

She was meant to say. *"Hickey, another chair!"*

Instead she stared blankly into space.

Oh, God. What I dreaded most had happened. Her memory had failed. I should've told Dad. I should've warned him.

Angus coughed again. "Whuff-whuff-whuff! Aghhh! "

"Hickey, another chair," I whispered from the wings.

Nothing.

She looked even more vacant. What was wrong?

192

It was my fault. Dad could've got someone else.

"*Hickey, another chair,*" I hissed again.

The audience shifted restlessly.

Angus looked desperate. Why didn't he improvise?

Luckily I couldn't see Dad's face at the back of the theatre.

"*Hickey another chair!*" I prompted again in desperation.

Then Bentley jumped in with, "I'll bring another chair!"

This seemed to jolt Ivy out of her torpor. She said her next line and the play picked up.

"I'm sorry," she mouthed, as she came off.

"It was fine," I whispered back, "no one noticed."

You could rely on Bentley. He was a real puzzle. Why had he acted like that during the rehearsals? He had saved the night so far. Thanks to him we got to the first act curtain without any more glitchs.

When it went down, everyone clapped.

Then streamed out to the lobby, laughing.

Actually laughing.

Had we a hit?

Would Dad's last turkey be a new beginning? A start for all the young people – Katie, Shay, Jerry? Would it resurrect Ivy from the ashes and pull Fidelma from the suburban doldrums, launch Angus as a professional and revive Oliver's flagging career as a redundant singing soap-opera star?

During the interval I helped Aunt Brigid serve coffee. She was in her element – all rouge and lace.

"Café!" she shrieked. "Café!"

A few people lingered to order it. But the Pigsty had a tiny lobby, so most spilled down the stairs and out onto grimy Talbot Street. A few stood outside the theatre. But most streamed over to the Plough pub opposite the Abbey Theatre.

Dad stood nervously in the lobby. "Try and flog the coffee, Clare!" he whispered. "It might be hard to get them back from the pub."

This was true.

"Coffee?" I called frantically, as the last of our audience wandered out and down the stairs. "Coffee's being served in the lobby."

No one stopped.

I stood in the theatre doorway, but couldn't staunch the flow. "Bewley's coffee! The best Columbian beans!"

Our life-blood was gone, to be lost in the crush of Talbot Street and the warm acrid night.

Back in the lobby, Aunt Brigid was shakily filling cups. I got one for Grandad, who sipped it in a group with Heather and Shay's ma. They were chatting animatedly about their offspring. He looked as if he was at a funeral.

"Enjoying it, Grandad?" I asked nervously.

He nodded grimly, shakily holding his coffee.

I remembered he'd had a cold. "You're looking better."

"I'm feeling terrible," he grumped.

I waited for him to say there were three stages in life. But he didn't.

"Grandad hates you to say he's looking well," I whispered to Shay's ma.

"You're lookin' terrible, Grandad!" She thumped his back, laughing raucously.

He was so startled, he almost dropped his cup. Coffee was slopped in his saucer, so I got him another.

"He needs a good slap!" Mrs Connors thumped him again.

God.

While Heather giggled, I waited nervously. In a minute

there'd be an explosion. But Grandad just humphed, smiled, and took fresh coffee. Smiled? It was amazing. Was he sweet on Mrs Connors? He looked it. Maybe we'd been treating him the wrong way for all these years? Maybe we should've occasionally given him a good slap on the back – shock treatment?

"Whan are ye due?" Mrs Connors asked Heather, and they got talking about the baby. Heather said she loved girls and was glad to be having another.

"Yez'll have yer hands full," she said to me.

I nodded resignedly.

"Isn't Ivy wonderful?" Heather then changed the subject. "And Shay has a career in front of him."

Mrs Connors glowed with pride. "Yez're good to take him on. Katie's good too."

It was Heather's turn to be proud.

"Shay's very talented, Mrs Connors," she said. "Dan talks about him all the time."

Mrs Connors looked about to burst. "Sure they're all fuckin' wonderful!"

Even Grandfather smiled. Aunt Brigid came over then and grabbed his cup, "I'll take that, Alex!"

He held it firmly. "I'm not finished!"

"Now give her that!" Mrs Connors took it jocosely.

I waited again for an explosion but Grandad again smiled weakly. He stared at her in fascination. If only he wasn't so old, they might have a fling.

"It's time to take your seats!" Aunt Brigid ordered, piling the used cups and saucers up behind the small counter.

"Come on, Mr Fitzgerald!" Mrs Connors took Grandad's arm.

He limped back with her, while Heather waited in the

lobby. She was going back early to Bray to prepare the party for the cast.

It was time for the curtain to go up. But most of our audience were still in the damn pub.

Hell – what was keeping them?

"We've got to get 'em back!" Dad wailed.

I looked out to the street. No one there belonged to us. "How?"

He was desperate. "Go tell 'em!"

So I ran across to the Plough, announcing from the door, "The Pigsty curtain's going up!"

The lounge was crowded. Men hovered at the bar.

"Everyone! The Pigsty curtain's going up!"

The barman gave me a funny look.

I ran over to the counter. "Will you tell them our interval's over!"

He wouldn't announce it. So I ran around the pub, telling anyone who looked like our audience that they had to take their seats.

Finally people began to straggle back – in ones and twos and threes. I waited in the street, herding them in as if they were lost sheep. "Hurry, please! The curtain's going up."

At last they were all back.

We hadn't lost any.

Then I went backstage again, praying: Oh, dear God, let us be a success. For our dad's sake, for Luke's – although he'd go back to his university job in America. But we needed to be a success. For Dad. For our new life in Bray . . . For Heather and the new baby, for all the actors . . . Oh, God, please.

The second act curtain finally went up – fifteen minutes late.

The play opened with a funny chat-up scene between Jerry

and Shay as Tennessee and Art talking at cross purposes – one a country hick and the other a city-slick gay. Art thinks Tennessee's propositioning him:

Tennessee: Ya know I'm delighted with this opportunity.
Art: Wha?
Tennessee: Well, I wanted to get with ya.
Art: Oh. Well, I don't mind, when?
Tennessee: Well, uh, now.
Art: You're out of your mind. That'd burn Hickey up.

They were great.

The audience howled.

Absolutely howled.

Were we a hit?

But then everything changed – Fidelma came on.

Fidelma and Ben, as Shirley Temple O'Shea and T Boyle O'Malley took up most of the second act. Fidelma throws her tantrum, and he then sacks the whole cast because she falls out of love with him. Then at the last minute she saves the play by persuading him to change his mind and go ahead with the production.

Shirley Temple was feisty, which Fidelma was in real life – very much so. Yet now, just as in rehearsal, she couldn't seem to act it.

Her accent was flat and faked.

If only she'd just been herself, acted the way she behaved that day in the fur coat shop.

But no.

She swaggered on, in outrageous curly yellow wig, fur coat trailing to her ankles, but ignoring Dad's careful blocking. And her voice was absolutely dead:

Now, hear this, everybody! I've been waiting around all

morning for you bit players to get it together, and if you
ask me you're all just a bunch of first-class egotists . . .
She got through the speech. She was as funny as a wet Friday.

I could hear yawns in the audience.

Dad's fuming seemed to electrify the air.

The play-within-the-play had flopped. With Fidelma's
entrance, ours too seemed to deflate like a punctured tire. The
air hissed out of it the minute Fidelma came on. Nothing
could inject any more life into it – until the old people came
back again at the end of the second act and looked around at
the old theatre, lamenting that their play is being abandoned:

Pembroke: It's . . . a nice old theatre.

Perdita: Yes. Oh, yes, lovely.

Slowly they collected their things, and Perdita helped
Pembroke into his coat. Finally they were ready to leave the
theatre for the last time. There was a silence in our theatre – a
great respect for Ivy.

Pembroke: Remember the first time we played here? In
'26, in Oscar's *Importance*? You were Cecily.

Perdita: You were Jack. But it was in '27.

Pembroke: Yes. '26.

Perdita: That was Romeo.

Pembroke: Hah, you were Juliet!

Suddenly Pembroke became the sprightly young Romeo.

He jests at scars that never felt a wound!
But soft! What light from yonder window breaks?
It is the east, and Juliet is the sun.

Then he snapped his fingers, desperately trying to remember.

Pembroke: I can't remember.

Perdita: It is my lady . . .

Pembroke: It is my lady, O, it is my love!

Our whole house remained entranced as the old actors

198

reminisced about former glorious days. It didn't matter if they forgot anything, because they were meant to be at the end of their acting lives anyhow. They were both completely in character and completely held the audience. There was a really relaxed atmosphere in the theatre. It was magic.

Then Fidelma stamped back on, breaking the spell.

> Come on you guys! Come on, snap it up! Get your butts back in here . . .

It was hard to float with a stone around your neck.

When the curtain finally fell, there was clapping. The actors took their bows, Ivy getting the longest and loudest applause. She accepted it like some ancient and much-loved queen, hardly ever seen by her subjects but loved the more so for that.

Katie grinned like a kid.

And the two boys.

I gave Ivy a bunch of flowers.

After the second curtain call, Dad came backstage. I knew by his face that he wasn't happy. But he thanked all the actors graciously, "Thanks guys. It was great."

I noticed he didn't look at Fidelma.

Now everything depended on the press.

Chapter Seventeen

After locking up the Pigsty, Dad, Luke, Katie and I took the last DART back to Westfield Park for our first night party. Luckily we had that to take our mind off the reviews. We had no matching delph, but perhaps no one would notice. The house looked great. There was a bedroom for coats. I'd washed the curtains and cut the grass, spent the morning on last minute tidying and making egg and salad sandwich filling. As I said, Heather'd gone ahead to get things started.

Aunt Brigid had wanted to come, but with Mabel gone, Grandfather had no transport and was too mean to pay a taxi. It was a pity. But the others all got out somehow, either by car, taxi or train. Even Ivy came, driven by Angus who also brought his wife – a horsy type, in heavy tweed skirt and twinset. Then Bentley appeared at the door with two young long-haired girlfriends – they were about Katie's age and so mannequin thin that I couldn't help staring.

What did they see in him?

Not one, but two?

Oliver brought his wife, a cosy, plump person. And Fidelma her famous journalist husband. I recognised him at once from the TV show, *Questions and Answers*, on which he sometimes appeared as a panellist for right wing causes. We didn't have a TV, but I remember Grandad had particularly objected to his ties. He wore a trendy pink shirt now which matched the pink of his face. The tie complemented both. He was arrogant but not bad-looking, except for his drinker's face. What did he see in his wife? But then love was a queer duck.

I knew that.

Our little house buzzed. A party of happy people was something I'd always imagined having. Heather had made the sandwiches, and Luke and Dad had bought the wine and beer, with assorted soda for any non-drinkers – Dad basically. My one dread was that he'd go back on the bottle if we got bad reviews.

But he seemed calm. He poured his usual pint glass of diet Coke. Katie, of course, was allowed wine, and Heather was so sick these days that she couldn't even drink coffee. Not that she'd drink alcohol, even if she felt like it, as it was bad for the baby. The baby was a lifebuoy someone had thrown her. Dad was the same about the play.

Some of the actors spilled out into the garden which was coolish in the summer night. But a full moon flooded it with light. I passed round a plate of egg sandwiches, stopping at Katie and Jerry who were wrapped round each other under the straggly apple tree.

"Here." I held out the plate. "Food!"

They took some sandwiches, which Katie munched nervously. "Was I OK?"

I'd told her she was, several times, on the DART. "You were great. So were you, Jerry. We have to wait and see."

"'Did you hear about the stupid hitch-hiker who set out early to miss the traffic?'" my sister quipped nervously.

God, she was at it again. Was it ominous? Would we miss the traffic?

I moved away.

Shay was behind them in a flowing white shirt and tennis shoes. It was warm, but he wore his usual baseball cap with the pony-tail sticking out. He stepped up and took a sandwich which he ate hungrily. "Tanks, Clare. Uses up a lot of calories – all that actin'."

I lingered beside him. "Your ma enjoyed herself."

His face softened. "Yeah, she doesn't get many nights out."

"She hit it off with Grandfather."

Shay laughed. "Did she?"

"She was certainly able for him." I grimaced. "He's tough."

He shook his head. "So's she! Hasta be!"

As he munched, I wondered would anything ever happen between us? He hadn't brought a girl to the party. Did that mean he was with me? He was always friendly but detached. But it was selfish to think such thoughts on such a night.

Bentley was huddled with his harem. "Clah, Clah! Over here!"

I went over.

"I've worked up an appetite."

That was nothing new.

As he grabbed a handful of sandwiches, I passed the plate to the two anorexics. "Take a supply. I'm making more."

They took the rest, smiling vapidly.

I watched them eating, wondering again about Bentley. He seemed so normal now with his beautiful willowy women. Could he really have wanted to sabotage us? It didn't make sense. But then who had done it? What was he doing with an axe? He had a fireplace OK, but did he chop wood for it?

"Well, what is it?" he quizzed over his wire glasses.

"Eh – nothing." I went red.

"You're too quiet, Clah."

"You were all great," I said, which was true. "Congratulations."

Everyone was, except Fidelma – despite Dad's careful teaching, she'd just never got it. Blocking, emphasis, anything.

Then I got courage to confront Bentley. "Everything went OK. Despite the break-in. Wonder who did it?"

He just shrugged. "It was pwetty pointless. Dublin's getting rough."

I nodded – he certainly didn't act guilty.

"Eh – we called up to see you – Shay and I. To tell you rehearsals were off."

He looked curious. "So it was you! Mrs Murphy said someone called."

"She *insisted* we go in and wait."

"Well, I should hope so. Thanks, Clah. It was very nice of you guys."

No, he hadn't done it. We'd been terrible.

From inside came the sound of Oliver's tenor voice:

"I dream of Jeanie with the light brown hair . . ."

This time it wasn't crisis intervention. He loved singing and now had an audience. The sound wafted over the night, adding an air of melancholy. Of lost love. Of summer's end.

Back in the kitchen, Heather and I made more sandwiches, listening as he sang several verses. Luke sat at the table, smoking and sipping coffee from a mug. I guessed it was spiked as always.

"Well, how'd it go?" I asked Luke – stupid, because I knew the answer.

He gulped his drink. "Fine . . . until the second act."

I didn't know what to say. So I brought more sandwiches into the dingy drawing-room with its dark, worn, old-lady furniture. Fidelma was sitting on the couch, looking around patronisingly.

"What a cute house, Clare!" she screamed. "Is it really called Haworth?"

"Yes. And thanks." I was embarrassed. Did she mean it?

She smiled falsely. Her eyes were outlined blackly and she reeked of expensive perfume. "Pity it isn't somewhere else."

I was taken aback. "But we love Bray."

She curled her lip. "Too many fish and chippers. It's like Blackpool."

I'd never been there. But if it was anything like Bray, it must be OK. Bray had hurdy-gurdies and fresh fish and chips. Hadn't she ever walked up to the head? Out the Cliff Walk to Greystones? Noticed the gorse on the Sugar Loaf? Although that was burnt off now, as there'd been fires all summer. Bray was home. The sight of children playing with buckets and spades was like an old song in your head. A song Heather had sung years ago: "Long time ago, long time, passing . . ."

"We're not long here . . ." I muttered.

How much longer, if our play didn't take off?

Already we were late with this month's rent. A solicitor had called for it. The ESB bill was due. What would become of us if we had to leave? What would become of Heather and the baby? Would the family of Kelly ever engage the general good opinion of their surrounding acquaintance? We had to make money. You couldn't live on fresh air. The reviews had to be good.

"How was the play, Clare?" Fidelma snapped.

I felt awkward.

"How were we?" she barked. "Come on!"

I repeated Luke's comment about the second act, almost biting my tongue off, realising what I'd said.

She was outraged. "But that's when *I'm* on."

"I know."

204

Aquarians are bluntly honest, which was sometimes a great disadvantage to me, particularly now. But there was no taking it back.

She stared at me, in a sort of shock.

I cowered mentally, expecting verbal blows. But she just whispered rather sadly, "Are you *sure*, Clare?"

"They took ages to come back from the pub. We shouldn't have had an interval," I blurted.

"Was that it?" She looked relieved, worriedly sipping wine.

Then Ivy floated over from another conversation. She was all flowing lilac robes and wore a matching bow in her hair, which was weirdly youthful. She sat creakily down beside us. "That's better. I'm not good late at night. The legs give out."

"Have an egg sandwich?" I passed the plate.

She took one. "Thank you, darling."

"Was I terrible, Ivy?" Fidelma was chewing a nail now.

I suppose even an atom bomb can be vulnerable.

"Clare says we flopped in the second act."

Ivy nibbled politely on her sandwich. "Everyone did their best, dear."

Ivy personified that brave spirit of the theatre. Dad did also. Both were dedicated warriors in the battle against philistinism.

The party went well.

I had a déjà-vu feeling. Although the first ever for the Kelly family, it seemed to have happened before, long ago in my childhood, before all the sad years and before Dad left. But maybe that was my imagination. Even if it didn't happen before, it was happening now. We were a family again.

The older people didn't stay late.

Finally Shay and Jerry hitched a ride back to Dublin with Fidelma and her husband. But Bentley and his harem sat

205

around till the small hours, eating and drinking everything in the house, including all the breakfast coffee. Finally Luke put them in a taxi, paid the fare to Synge Street and we all went to bed.

I got a few hours sleep.

As usual, Dad's Al Jolson singing awoke me.

The sun shines east, the sun shines west . . .

Heather was long gone to work and Dad was frowning over the papers as I wandered sleepily into the kitchen.

All was not well – I knew at once.

He looked up. "Ah, Clare . . ."

I was nervous. "What's it say?"

He laughed shortly, passing the *Times* to me. "It's not going to fill many seats."

I scanned it:

> . . . It was good to see such talented old hands as Ivy Biscovitcz back on the Dublin stage – older theatre-goers will remember her from the Gate. As always she impressed with her great clarity and presence. There were also some fine and intelligent performances from the newcomers in the cast, particularly Shay Connors and Katie Kelly. It is just a pity the playwright couldn't come up with a better vehicle for their talent. Luke Merrill's comedy is slickly American, reminiscent of *Roseanne* on an off-day. On top of that, the play started late and there was an unnecessarily long interval. No doubt this was to pad out an already too slight script. The members of the audience who could overlook this insult might have accepted that the discomfort of the venue was part of the play's atmosphere. But this critic was not so forgiving . . .

What was he talking about?

How could he say that about Luke's lovely play? The writing wasn't remotely like *Roseanne* – on a off-day or any other. And we were late at the interval because the audience *wouldn't* come back. Was it our fault if The Pigsty had hard seats?

It was unfair. Still Katie and Shay had got a mention.

Dad was perusing the *Independent*. "Hmm. This is a bit better. 'The humour is original but often descended to the slapstick. It would be a help if Ivy Biscovicz could have remembered her lines . . . Surely, there comes a time for us all to retire . . .'"

Dad rustled the paper furiously. "Ivy was fine! We were fine until Fidelma messed things up."

"Has Luke seen them?" I asked.

Dad stared gloomily into his coffee. "Yeah, he's gone for a walk on the front."

I read the two reviews again. "Maybe they aren't so bad?"

Dad jumped up. "They're terrible. But the evening paper might be better. And I can take a few quotes from these to advertise. 'Original humour' . . . 'the great Ivy Biscovicz returns to the Dublin stage,'" he scribbled on a pad. "Go back to bed now, Clare. You had a late night. I'll call Fidelma. We'll have a short rehearsal this afternoon."

I never admired him more.

At life's lowest moment he'd still be trying.

Dad went into town and after a bowl of cereal, I went back to bed and read *Tales of Avonlea*. Lucy Maud Montgomery had comforted me in many a storm.

Katie, of course, snored obliviously.

There was definitely something wrong with her adenoids.

207

In all of life's crises, she slept. Nothing ever disturbed her. She'd be snoring if Sellafield blew up. Or a third world war declared. Or if the floods came. Or the planet were conquered by creatures from outer space. I could just picture her yawning sleepily at the little green Martians, "Oh, where did you come from?" Then going back to sleep.

I fell back to sleep myself.

At noonish I went back into the kitchen where Luke was sitting over a coffee and the papers. "Hi, Clare. You've seen these?"

"Yeah." I put on the kettle. "They're stupid."

He shrugged resignedly. "Can't win 'em all. According to GBS, 'Success is the end of everything and should be put off till one's funeral.'"

It was the second good quote I'd heard from that writer.

I started to prepare lunch. "Dad's using some quotes for a newspaper ad."

He smiled, shaking his head. "Your Dad's one hell of a guy."

I had to admit it, Dad kept his head. He met with triumph and disaster and treated the impostors just the same. A pity it was mostly disaster.

After lunch I went into town and spent the afternoon handing out fliers for the play in O'Connell Street. People acted like I was giving out information on brothels. It was an awful job, and I swore never to refuse to take one in future. Then I went round the hotel lobbies and begged the porters to take some and direct visitors to our play.

Dad was right – the *Herald* was kinder. That critic thought it was "a lovely play with delightful characters and just the sort of thing for a summer's evening."

She had some sense.

I felt better able to face the actors.

Ivy was waiting at the door of the Pigsty as I arrived to unlock it that evening. As usual she'd come dressed for her part and looked more regal than ever in her big black veiled hat and trailing robes.

I handed her the *Herald*.

She put on reading glasses and scanned it. "Hmm, an improvement on the two idiots this morning."

"How do you stand all the criticism?" I pushed open the door.

She was philosophical. "I'm used to it, darling."

"I couldn't stand it!"

"Then you can't be a pilgrim, darling."

"A pilgrim?"

As we creaked up the stairs, her wobbly old voice sang:

> Who would true valour see
> Let him come hither.
> One here will constant be
> Come wind, come weather.
> There's no discouragement
> Shall make him once relent
> His first avowed intent
> To be a pilgrim.

It was beautiful. Why didn't Catholics have hymns like that?

"The journey matters, darling. Not the arrival."

I admired her so much.

She looked right in my face, then grabbed my hand. "Now, come and have some cake! I've made one for the cast."

It was a big chocolate sponge. And each cast member was offered a slice as they appeared in the cramped dressing-room. All took it, except Fidelma who was counting calories.

While the others were eating, she pulled me to one side. "Clare, I want you to do me a favour."

I nodded cautiously. Did she want me to set up another date with Jerry?

"I want you to make me angry."

"What?"

"Say things to me before I go on."

"What?" was all I could say.

She thumped me gently. "Stop saying *what!*"

"OK."

"I want you to call me names!"

I hesitated. "Like *bitch*?"

She nodded, then someone came over.

"Will you do that, Clare?" she pleaded when they'd gone.

Nervously I agreed.

There was an atmosphere of camaraderie, of being bloodied but unbowed by the morning papers. So perhaps something might yet be retrieved. All was not lost. The day might yet be won.

Then I noticed Jerry hadn't eaten his cake and just sat mournfully with a hand over his mouth.

"What is it?" I asked.

"I lost me front tooth," he said in his Cork lilt.

"Where?"

"Got knocked off de bike."

That very morning, while cycling around the Green, he'd come across some people making a film. He was so distracted that he didn't look where he was going and accidentally bumped into a parked car. Of course, he'd been thrown over the handlebars. And snap went his front tooth.

He smiled like a big toothless kid. "Your Dad's paying for a new crown."

"What?" It was another case of men working. "But don't you have stamps or anything?"

He shook his head.

Couldn't his own dad pay?

Because of the *Herald*'s good review, a few people trickled in for the second night. We had no interval. We were doing great until the second act. This time things went wrong before Fidelma's entrance. At Jerry and Shay's chatting-up scene:

There was raucous laughter, as they talked at cross purposes – Jerry's character not realising that Shay's was making a pass at him. Then the whole front row got up and tramped noisily out.

What was wrong with them?

They looked like a big family up from the country.

Damn.

But it was time to goad Fidelma into anger.

"You're a bitch!" I whispered in the wings as we both awaited her cue.

She started breathing heavily. "What did you say?"

Hell, didn't she remember she had asked me to do this. "You're a bitch. B-I-T-C-H!"

She looked as if I'd slapped her.

"Your suntan's fake!"

"It is not!"

"Fake! And you tried to steal Jerry!"

That got her. She went on and was much better. A new woman.

At the last curtain, the remaining customers clapped loudly. Now all we needed was a bigger audience. But the morning papers had done their bit.

The country family waited in the lobby, demanding their money back – nearly all the takings. The reference to homosexuality had offended them.

Amazing.

Aunt Brigid had refused, but Dad didn't hesitate.

I gestured frantically at him not to, but he went on counting out the money.

Was he completely crazy?

Despite my glares, he blandly handed it over.

As they left, he said, "You have to, Clare."

I didn't think so. "Could I give back a meal half-eaten?"

He shrugged. "There's no point in arguing with people."

"Could you demand your licence money back, if there was something you didn't like on TV?"

He paid no attention.

But there was more to come.

On the DART home, Dad was uncharacteristically glum.

I tried to cheer him, remembering Ivy's spirit. "It'll pick up, Dad."

He looked gloomy. "The weather's against us, as well as reviews."

I never knew good weather prevented people going to plays. The train trundled on and we were in the middle of the Dalkey tunnel when Dad announced. "There's something else, Clare."

I sensed it was awful. "What?"

"You might as well know."

"What?"

He looked miserable. "Mabel wasn't stolen."

I didn't know what he meant. "What?"

212

He put his head despairingly in his hands. "I have to tell you!"

"But, what?" Then it hit me. "You didn't *sell* Mabel?"

He sort of squirmed in front of me. "No."

"Well, what then?

"She's hocked. Now I don't know if we'll be able to get her back."

God.

"But what about Grandfather?"

Dad shrugged helplessly.

Two may be the magic number, but disaster hits in threes and fours and fives. The worst thing had happened now – my da was a criminal too.

Chapter Eighteen

Mabel was the last Mohican. It was the first night of my soul. I'd lost all my illusions. Dad was a thief. He was no better than Shay's da. But one thing obsessed me – had Heather known? I had tried to understand my parents. To forgive them for dumping us with Grandfather all those years. To realise that real life could never equal their impossible dreams. That for them hope outpaced reality. But Mabel finished me.

This was THE END.

I'd had it.

Grandfather was difficult. But you could love a mean old fart. Even a right wing old looney. That Dad had raised the money for the play from a money lender, using Mabel as security, was surely just not true? It couldn't be. But it was. He thought Grandfather was too old to drive, and that gave him the right to confiscate his car. But I couldn't stop wondering if Heather'd had anything to do with it? I thought so. She was irresponsible too and had done something like this once before – with a painting. To pay for us to go to London for a summer two years back. That had been sorted out, but could this be? After all the police were involved, as Dad had reported the theft. How was he going to get out of this one? The parents were livin' dolls with wooden hearts, like the old songs they were always singing.

At home I faced Dad. "But you went to the police? You could be up for fraud – giving false information."

He looked away. "I didn't report it."

I was sick. "You just gotta funny feeling! Remember?"

He still couldn't look at me. But that's what he'd said, I remembered. It was all a sham. He'd faked the theft to fund his egotistical artistic schemes.

All night I tossed and turned, unable to sleep. My whole life flashed before me. I now saw everything clearly for the first time ever. Grandfather was a saint, not a penny-pinching Ayatollah. He had always picked up the tab for Dad. For years he had looked after us, while they drank Guinness and guzzled oysters in Dublin and then London. He looked after Aunt Brigid too, although he got no thanks for that either. Now he was an old man with only a nursing home to look forward to. It wasn't fair.

How could Dad have done it? His car was Grandfather's pride and joy. His one pleasure in life. Was any play worth stealing for? Dad was a common thief.

It was shocking.

The night after Heather's hospital test, the night when they said Mabel was stolen, she had acted the innocent, pretending to have asthma.

I was miserable.

Miserable.

It seemed I had just nodded off when Dad's usual breakfast noise awoke me.

I stumbled out of bed, tiptoeing past Katie. As usual, she was snoring peacefully – she didn't know. It was always me. But I preferred it like that. She'd only worry.

215

In the kitchen Dad was eating quite cheerfully, while reading the paper. "Hi, Clare."

I didn't answer.

He went on eating and frowning over the news.

I put on the kettle.

"There's coffee made," he said brightly.

I snapped on the radio.

Although I loved coffee, *he* had made it. I was finished with him.

The news was over, so I flicked the radio off.

Dad rustled the newspaper again. I now saw him as he was – a thief. Oscar Wilde was right about parents and children. I now judged Dad and would never forgive him. Heather maybe, but not him. Ever.

Finally Dad cleared his throat as if to say something. He blinked innocently. "There's no need to act like that."

I glared. "How'm I supposed to act?"

He threw down the newspaper. "I wish you wouldn't judge me, Clare."

"You *stole* Grandad's car!"

He sighed heavily. "*Borrowed* it."

"Without permission. That's stealing. Did Heather know?"

"No." He scraped his plate at the sink.

That was a relief. "You're sure?"

"Yes. Now, stop worrying."

"I suppose I'm to tell Grandfather?"

"No. We'll get it back. Luke's got a credit card."

It wasn't fair on Luke, but I was relieved all the same.

"He can get cash," Dad went on. "We can redeem Mabel."

"Today?"

He nodded. "I'm meeting him at the bank. I'll bring the car back to Ranelagh this afternoon. You can come with us."

216

But suddenly I was angry again. "Handy, isn't it?"

"What?"

"Luke being here."

He looked amazed that I was saying this, but I didn't care. "All our life Grandad bailed you out. Now Luke."

Dad held up his hand. "Please, Clare –"

"Why don't you grow up? Isn't it about time to show some maturity?" Then the resentments of years flowed out of me. "You left us. You walked off. We didn't know where you were for years."

I started crying.

He paled and stood beside me, not knowing what to do.

I couldn't help myself. "Katie couldn't remember what you looked like. She'd probably be a delinquent, if Grandfather hadn't been so good with her."

He frowned in puzzlement. "A delinquent?"

Didn't he ever count his cigarettes? Smell her breath after a night out? "She had problems."

He was still baffled. "Problems? How was he good with her?"

"He was there!"

This got him. "I'm here now, Clare."

I stopped.

He seemed actually ashamed. "I was desperate, Clare. Have you never done anything you regret?" he asked in a low voice.

I didn't answer him.

Grandad was right. He was a no good. A selfish layabout who thought he was some sort of artistic genius. Well, he wasn't. He was just like everyone else in the whole damn world. I didn't care if he left us. I was leaving home and taking Katie with me. Heather and the baby could come too. I was sick of hoping for things to be normal. They'd never be with him. Maybe we could live in a caravan somewhere, like Ivy.

Then Heather came in.

Oddly she was still in her dressing-gown and looked deadly pale. It was unlike her not to be dressed. I thought she must've known and felt guilty. I was just about to accuse her, when she said quietly, "Call an ambulance, Clare."

We both stared in shock.

"What?" I was worried now.

She looked absolutely dreadful. "I think I'm losing the baby."

I ran to her, while Dad tore out to the phone.

Suddenly nothing mattered but Heather's baby. Why had I been so unwelcoming to my new sister? If you think something, can it happen? I hadn't wanted her to be born. I felt so guilty. If she was lost, it'd be nemesis like the Greeks were always writing about. It seemed an eternity till the ambulance came. It screeched to a stop outside the house in about fifteen minutes. Heather was taken to hospital. I wanted to go with her, but Dad went instead. If Heather miscarried, it was his fault. Everything was.

Heather didn't miscarry. Katie and I brought her in nighties that evening. The ward was full of women. I got a déjà vu feeling. Heather had been in hospital before, except they were other kinds of hospitals. This hospital was a place of hope, of new beginnings.

As a woman in another bed breastfed her baby, I saw my new sister taking her first wobbly steps toward me, hands held out. Why had I been so mean?

Heather's eyes were wrinkled, her hair lank. "It's OK now."

I couldn't say anything to upset her.

But I still didn't speak to Dad.

And Mabel?

Well, Luke got the money to retrieve her the day after Heather's scare. I went with them to get her. I had to see that Mabel was undamaged and delivered safely home. On the way Luke tried to get me to talk to Dad, but I wouldn't budge. He took us into Bewleys for coffee. We found a table in the smoking section and Dad asked me what I wanted.

I didn't answer. From now on I was asserting myself.

Dad paled in anger. "Clare, answer me!"

I wouldn't – although people were looking.

Dad fumbled for a cigarette. His face twitched ominously. He was in my face. "You know your problem, young woman?"

He was going to say I hadn't been slapped enough – I knew. A pity he was so busy slapping Heather.

"You've been corrupted by feminists!"

That was a good one.

"Feminist nuns!" he ranted.

"Oh, Dan!" Luke sighed.

I was the only feminist I knew. A generation had stood by and watched while people were killed in camps in the Second World War. We did it in History. But I wasn't prepared to stand by and see Grandfather's car being stolen.

Luke butted in kindly, "Whatja havin', Clare?"

"A mug of white coffee and a cherry bun," I snapped.

"A mug of white coffee and a cherry bun," he repeated emphatically to Dad. "I'll have black coffee and an almond bun."

Dad nodded curtly and went off.

While he was getting it, Luke lectured me. "I don't think your attitude's helpful, Clare. He made a mistake."

I held firm. "Look, I'm *never* speaking to Dad again."

219

Luke sighed. "That'll be difficult with the actors."

"The play'll be over soon." It had picked up a bit the last two nights. We were getting small audiences, but not filling the theatre.

Luke was patient. "You'll still be a family."

"We'll never be a *normal* family."

He lit a cigarette. "There's no such thing as a normal family."

I didn't answer immediately. "What do you mean?"

"There are only imperfect families."

"Have you not noticed he's irresponsible?"

"He hoped, Clare. Then got carried away. Can't you understand, he was desperate?"

"Frankly, no!"

Luke inhaled deeply. "It was my fault too. I shouldn't have let him do it. You know how Warner Brothers got their start? They pawned their father's horse."

I humphed. "With his permission?"

Then Dad came back. Grimly he passed me my stuff. "Here, Clare."

I took it without thanking him.

He concentrated on talking to Luke.

Afterwards we went to a garage off the South Circular Road. An odd-looking character opened the big double doors. There was all sorts of junk there, but way at the back, there was Mabel – shiny and blue and in perfect health. The wide front ventilator sort of smiled at you.

Luke handed over a wad of money. The man counted it discreetly. Then backed Mabel out. Everything looked intact – even her lovely red stripe.

Thank God for that.

How could Dad have done it?

We got in. The motor jerked to spluttering life. It coughed chestily, then started. We drove her to Ranelagh, chugged into Grandfather's road, and home at full throttle.

You should've seen Grandfather's face.

He tottered out to the front garden gate, looking proudly at his plucky little car with its bull-like shoulders and wheezy engine. "Dan, you found it? How amazing!"

Dad blinked. "They often turn up completely unscratched." He was a good actor.

Aunt Brigid fussed around, exclaiming in French. Grandad made us all come in for a cup of tea and his rock-like scones. Then he actually said he enjoyed the play, and had totally disagreed with the critics.

Dad went red. "Thank you, sir."

"Yes," the old man said in an amazed way, "I've never laughed so much in my life."

That was probably true. He hardly ever laughed.

And the play? We struggled on for a week. Everyone was great, even Fidelma, thanks to my goading. I got good at saying nasty things. But we had to close. It was sad. It always is when a curtain goes down. But despite the fliers and an ad in the papers, there was no way we could recover from the terrible reviews or the good weather. The play-within-our-play they had succeeded, thanks to T Boyle O'Malley, Oliver's character, coughing up the money. But life isn't art.

On the Sunday after we closed, Ivy gave a garden party and cooked a wonderful meal. Everyone came. All the cast, even Grandfather and Aunt Brigid. It was magic in that beautiful mystical garden.

But awkward. Although I acted normally for the performances, I still wasn't talking to Dad off-stage.

221

No one noticed, but Ivy.

Afterwards, I helped her clear up. She took me aside, whispering, "You're on the outs with Papa?"

I nodded. "I can't tell you why."

She patted my arm. "Parents behave badly. Then they're surprised when their children react. He looks very hurt, darling."

Was she taking his side?

"He's tried so hard with the play," she added. "It's been such a happy show."

I didn't think it was all that happy.

"You know what he did?" I blurted. "He pawned Grandfather's car to pay for it!"

I had said it.

She looked thoughtful. "Well, that was naughty. But quite honestly, darling, your grandfather shouldn't be driving. He's far too old."

Who'd believe it? "I'm never talking to him again!"

She lowered her eyes and her voice. "Now, Clare. Your father has fortitude, so you must have forgiveness."

I didn't agree, but felt better.

And the missing props? We found out who broke in.

One evening after we closed, Shay brought the deer's head out to Bray on the DART. He carried it up our garden path.

I was repelled by the sight of it. "Where'd you find it?"

"In a field behind the flats."

"Who took it?"

"The da. I'm pretty sure. The bastard hates me actin'."

"Where are the other props?"

He shrugged. "Fuckin' pawned maybe. Dunno."

I returned the head to the antique shop. Luckily they didn't say anything. Now we only had to worry about the bull fiddle, but the music academy are trying to claim it on their insurance. They think they'll be able.

Shay never said anything about us. So I finally made the first move.

I planned it all carefully. I bought new underwear in Dunnes and put on some of Heather's perfume. It was our six weeks "anniversary" of meeting, so I invited him out to Sunday afternoon tea. Heather was still in hospital and Dad was out. I had the house to myself.

As we sat on the couch listening to Katie's *Oasis* tapes, I leant over and kissed him on the lips.

"Clare!" Shay pulled away puzzled.

I kissed him again.

He laughed. "Yer a mad woman!"

I pulled out my condoms. "No, I'm not. Look!"

He looked puzzled for a minute, then chanted, "Be prepared! Be prepared!"

I went red. He didn't like me at all.

But he gave me a little hug. "You're the best girl I ever met, Clare. I'd love to marry ya."

"You would?"

"But I don't *like* girls."

I couldn't take it in. "You don't?"

He looked sad now. "Can I be the favourite uncle to your kids?"

I wasn't having any kids.

Then he hugged me again. "I'm gay, Clare. That's why me da hates me."

"Oh." I couldn't say anything.

At least my da didn't hate me.

My love came to nothing. The obvious had just never

223

occurred to me. All the time, I thought Shay was *acting* a gay. I felt sad for a while. Then it got better. All was not lost. I now had a buddy. And a buddy loved you – like Luke loved Dad. Dad was right – being a stage manager had taught me a lot. Mostly about human nature.

I never found out if Heather knew about Mabel. I couldn't worry her. She had to stay in bed for the rest of her pregnancy. By the way, she changed her mind about calling the baby Danielle. It's hard to say with Kelly, so she decided on Hope. Hope Mary Kelly is expected in a few months. She'll be our Christmas present – there won't be anything else.

I took over Heather's job in the book shop. They were a bit grumpy about losing her expertise. I knew nothing about Mills and Boon, but we had to eat.

Wally, my ex-boyfriend, came back from America and took me for a drink. I suppose we're a couple again. But more like brother and sister, so I'm still a eunuch. He looked tanned and even a bit muscular from clearing all those dishes. He had a crew cut and peered through round wire glasses.

"I'm rethinking Einstein, Clare."

"Oh . . ."

"He could've been wrong."

We all have our theories.

There was no big reconciliation scene with Dad. I just gradually spoke to him again.

I had to.

Otherwise, it'd just be a repetition of Heather and Grandfather. We'd had enough of that in our family. Mabel was a crime of passion. Maybe that's stretching it, but people went mad with hope – Dad for the play and Heather for the baby. It was all there was in life. Sometimes it carried people away. It was important to succeed, but more important to struggle. You needed that longing feeling. As Luke said, success was the end of everything. Hope was what mattered. It alone kept people going. Grandfather needed to hope more. He thought of nothing but dandelions.

No one was perfect. After all, I'd wanted Heather to miscarry. I'd been afraid of a little baby stealing the limelight. And I'd been jealous of Katie. Were they crimes worse than stealing? I'd forged an ID once, but had never stolen anything. Dad was so irresponsible it wasn't true. He was totally impractical. But generous to a fault.

One evening I tackled him about Jerry's tooth. "Why are you responsible?"

His eyebrows went up. "Had to help out there."

"I suppose Luke's paying for that too?"

"No. The dentist's giving credit." He looked weary. "I'm getting a real job, Clare. I promised, remember?"

I didn't believe him.

At the end of August, Luke had to go home to teach. He'd been our *Deus ex Machina*, saving everything at the last minute. But now he was out of money, having given all his to Dad. He still gave me a present – *The Complete Works of William Shakespeare*, inscribed with a "thank you" for all my work. It was very generous, considering he'd lost so much on the production.

Money remains a problem for us. We've got Dad's dole but it's not enough. Not the way he eats and drinks coke. And with Heather laid up.

So Dad actually kept his promise and got a job. It's still connected with the arts, but this time more practical. He

225

works all day in a bar and escorts tourists on a literary pub crawl in the evening. They meet outside Davy Byrne's pub every night.

He still isn't drinking.

And another thing, he's stopped dyeing his hair.

Nowadays he's to be seen nightly at the head of a little posse of visitors. He charges round Dublin, lecturing loudly as he goes. They visit all the literary haunts, then a group of actors do little scenes from the lives of Irish writers. And, as there's no shortage of them, he never runs out of material. Our cast are employed regularly – especially the young people.

Katie and Jerry are still an item and talking about marriage. I wish the parents would object, but they don't. Katie's too young. Anyway, she has two more years of school. And he's got into UCD to do Law. He'll be studying for years. When I told her that, she said to mind my own business.

I suppose nothing ever changes. But Jerry's been a good influence. Katie combs her hair now and doesn't run wild at cider parties. But she's gone back to the riddles.

I was going into Bewleys the other day and saw Bentley selling *The Big Issue* magazine outside. He told me he has another "gig" planned, but not in theatre.

"The theatre's dead, Clah," he said.

I said that'd be a sad day. Anyway it isn't true. With people like Dad around, it'll never die.

Shay was really launched by our play. He was offered a part in London's Bush Theatre. The play's by a new Irish writer and doing well. It got a write-up in the *Sunday Times*, mentioning him.

Dad hasn't taken me there yet.

But we go to the Dublin theatre on his night off. Lately we went to the Gate, where Angus and Fidelma were in a play.

The other good thing about our production was that Angus got an Equity card. He was great and Fidelma had nothing to do but sit, so she didn't have to worry about blocking. Another night we saw Ivy in a play at the Eblana. It got panned, of course, but I got a pain in my side laughing – that's just the way things go.

Oliver rings up now and again. He has the promise of a role in a new soap opera RTE are planning, but it hasn't got off the ground yet.

Ivy still invites me for a girls' lunch every so often.

Oh, the Leaving results came out. I got offered a place in UCD, for an Arts degree, but didn't get into the Beckett Centre. I ought to have known, when I wasn't recalled for another interview. But I suppose I'm like Dad in some things.

Grandfather was glad though. He even offered to cough up my university fees. But it's only for one year, as fees are being abolished. He grumbles that Aunt Brigid is out all the time now. She's taking acting lessons at the Gaiety School of Acting. Of course, she's the oldest in the class, but anything can happen in life. Heather's back buying Lotto tickets, and says our long term horoscopes are good. We come from the stars, after all, so maybe there's something in all her astrology. Maybe our number will come up. And someday I'll get an acting part. But I don't tell anyone about my hopes – just practise my diction.

Grandfather'd say I was turning out badly.